THE DARK SIDE OF KEY WEST

Enjoy!

RANDYMARY DEROSIER

THE DARK SIDE OF
KEY WEST

TATE PUBLISHING
AND ENTERPRISES, LLC

The Dark Side of Key West
Copyright © 2014 by Randymary deRosier. All rights reserved.

No part of this publication may be reproduced, stored in a retrieval system or transmitted in any way by any means, electronic, mechanical, photocopy, recording or otherwise without the prior permission of the author except as provided by USA copyright law.

This novel is a work of fiction. Names, descriptions, entities, and incidents included in the story are products of the author's imagination. Any resemblance to actual persons, events, and entities is entirely coincidental.

The opinions expressed by the author are not necessarily those of Tate Publishing, LLC.

Published by Tate Publishing & Enterprises, LLC
127 E. Trade Center Terrace | Mustang, Oklahoma 73064 USA
1.888.361.9473 | www.tatepublishing.com

Tate Publishing is committed to excellence in the publishing industry. The company reflects the philosophy established by the founders, based on Psalm 68:11,
"The Lord gave the word and great was the company of those who published it."

Book design copyright © 2014 by Tate Publishing, LLC. All rights reserved.
Cover design by Jim Villaflores
Interior design by Caypeeline Casas

Published in the United States of America

ISBN: 978-1-62994-456-2
1. Fiction / Mystery & Detective / General
2. Fiction / Medical
13.12.09

ACKNOWLEDGMENT

To my youngest sister, Kelly Ann deRosier, for her help with editing. Without her help I probably would not have sent it in for publication.

PREFACE

This tale starts at the Hotel Spanish Piece Duo, and what is about to be relayed may only be the start of the story.

To get a feeling for the hotel, stop by and survey a replica of the first hotel named Spanish Piece, whose structure was built in the turn of the century by a wealthy landowner for a summer retreat. After the owner died leaving no will, the building was left to the elements for many years, and it failed to the point of almost no return.

The second owner, Jac Scarin, bought the hotel for an investment and shortly after purchasing and restoring it, he watched as it burned to the ground over a competitor's revenge. Jac knew who had set the fire and why, but when the fire chief and his group came to investigate, they stated in the final report that it was faulty wiring not replaced during the renovation. That satisfied Jac for he knew in his mind that this problem he had to handle himself.

After receiving a tidy amount of cash in his last big business deal in Miami, Jac left that city for a more peaceful existence in the Florida Keys. The *family* business had finally gotten too big and too touchy for Jac's feeling of stability. Also, that old competitor and school chum was getting careless, and next time, someone would most likely die in one of his explosions.

Upon arriving at his property, Jac surveyed the burnt-out shell of his late hotel and decided to restore it bigger and better than the original Spanish Piece, including the grounds that needed a complete overhaul, and name it the Spanish Piece Duo. Finding the best architects and land developers, he instructed them to bring the hotel back to its original splendor, adding a beachside for the hotel, which he hoped would draw the interests of northern tourists. Jac's property had one of the nicest beachfronts in the area in which he added a marina, nine-hole golf course, and a gymnasium that held the latest Nautilus equipment money could buy. For the naturalists the grounds held several large exotic flower gardens which grew many well known plants of the tropics such as the amaryllis, desert rose, pomegranates, equadoriam rose, gardenia, oriental lily and, not to be forgotten, the bird of paradise. Finishing with an entrance approached with a circular drive that would take their breath away, starting from the main highway of the Indian Keys and Route 1, driving south from Miami.

Let's step back a few steps.

The last two years were disasters for Jac, both mentally and physically, for he struggled with deep depression, terrible pain from the bullets, and a deep hatred for the work he was doing; and so did Jac's past. With the help of a family member, a good body builder, and plastic surgery, the bullets that slammed into his face and body were finally healed, leaving a faint scar from below his left eye down to his once-shattered jaw. He was glad to be alive and started looking and feeling more like his productive self. Energized and out of the underworld that had caused him so much trouble three years before, Jac's mental state would have taken longer, but returning to his job/hobby of restoring broken lives would help. People who had gotten themselves into worse trouble than his past, that he could help resolve. So with the hotel's repairs coming to culmination, he decided he would leave the running of the hotel up to a manager and pursue his interests.

The hotel needed someone who can run it properly and is willing to stay longer than six months. In a year, his fourth manager had just given notice that he was returning to Miami for a more exciting life. This left him with two problems to solve—a new manager for the hotel and a solution for a small matter that was dogging at his heals. Unbeknown to Jac, his search was about to end in both areas.

CHAPTER

1

During the last two years, while living and working for a big hotel chain in Miami, KaSandra Martin found herself sick and tired of the rat race of putting in six days a week, ten to fifteen hours a day, as a hotel's manager with no time for a personal life. She took the advice from a friend to check out a job situated in the Keys, which could be just what she wanted. So, she quit her position and took the next bus from Miami to the Spanish Piece Duo.

Upon her arrival, she rang the front desk bell, and getting no answers to her hail, she decided to walk around to the bar area and see if she could get some help. Proceeding down the path to the beach, she noticed all the construction that was seemingly going on over her head and stopped to watch her curiosity abate when she reached the hotel's patio and bar area. Still seeing no one on duty, she looked further and found the hotel's gardens that were written up in the magazine *Gardens of America*. KaSandra, being an enthusiastic gardener, could not help herself from stopping to take a look. She noticed that even though the garden seemed cared for, she believed it could look better. The buds of most of the flowers were not as big and lush as the ones she had seen in the Caribbean. Even though the climate was the same, or better, since the keys got fewer bad storms, these blooms were several sizes smaller. After examining them more closely, she decided that they need a different fertilizer.

So engrossed in studying the plants, she did not notice that Jac had joined her at the entrance of the garden. "KaSandra Cassillian, you always were interested in gardening, but I did not expect to see you in mine." Seeing her jump in fright and put up a hand for protection, he quickly said, "Sorry, it's me, Kass, Jac Scarin from the old neighborhood."

KaSandra blinked several times and took several deep breaths to calm her heart and the adrenaline flow. Shielding her eyes from the sun, she found the person who had just used her name to be an old school mate, and that same person was the man she had once been very much in love with. "Jac, is it really you? What are you doing here?" was all that she could manage to say.

Laughing, Jac said, "Yes, it's me, Kass, and why are you standing in my hotel's garden?"

Looking over the property again, KaSandra spread her hands out in wonderment, saying, "This is your hotel? Well, I understood that this hotel was looking for a manager, and I'm here to claim the position."

Surprise showed on Jac's face for he did not expect Kass to say what she just did.

After recovering himself, he said, "Yes, it's mine, and it"s great to see an old face for a change! Are you serious about the manager's position? From what I had heard, you were doing so well up in Miami that nothing could have removed you from your position in that hotel chain."

"It really depends on what you're offering and what the hours are. The awful hours were one of the basic reasons I left the other job. Oh, Jac, from the looks of this place, are you even open for business?"

"Oh, the builders are only adding on the last floor and taking their time at it. I had a fire here not too long ago, and the building is now just getting its top floor, but it is very livable. Want a tour?"

"Yes, and while we walk, why don't you tell me what the job requires and when I start. By the way, my last name is Martin now and has been for the past five years even though I sometimes think of changing it back to Cassillian after all the trouble that rat fink, my ex, has put me through."

"Kass, is your ex-husband a member of the same Martin family that went to our school?"

"Yes, I married Paul Martin six years ago and divorced him a year later, and it's been like hell ever since. The man just won't give up. He says that I'm still his wife and no paper is going to change that. He is the other basic reason I left my job in Miami, without a forwarding address. If I can get far enough away, maybe I can find some peace."

As the two walked toward the hotel, Jac found he was only half listening to Kass talking about her ex-husband. He was watching the sheen on her hair under rays of the sun and the way her body swayed as she walked. She had changed a lot since they were in school together. Her stick-like body had filled out, and in its place were a nice curve and a firm-looking figure. Suddenly he heard her say, "Oh, Jac, it's nice to hear my nickname coming out of your mouth. No one has called me Kass since we were back in school."

"Right? That is probably because no one else ever dared to."

KaSandra laughed as they entered the hotel through the bar area for their tour. "Oh, come on. What do you mean?" said KaSandra.

"You know very well what I mean. The word rhymed with *ass*, and you didn't have one," said Jac. With that, Jac heard Kass's laughter echo throughout the unfinished hotel.

CHAPTER 2

Wow. KaSandra shook her head to release the direction her musing had been leading her. That day two years ago seemed like yesterday, she thought, sitting at her hotel desk for the last two hours, trying to do the accounting work, and still she hadn't gotten any further than when she started at 7:30. It was now 12:05, and she was thinking about taking the rest of the day off as she wasn't accomplishing anything from the work she had set for herself; it is still lying on the desk untouched.

KaSandra was twenty-nine years old, five eleven, and with auburn-blond hair that fell to her shoulders. A body that was rounded in the right places, with good full-looking breasts whose form showed through the cotton top, just enough to reveal their size. She also had a firm round fanny that swayed when she walks. The day was warm but not hot for February in the Florida Keys. KaSandra wore a mint-green cotton skirt with matching top that was sufficiently tight to show off her nice figure. The skirt flowed from the waist down and ended around the calf of her very long legs. A red scarf around her neck, a red Gucci shoulder bag, and a pair of red Manolo sandals added just the bright accent that the outfit needed.

Starting to walk down the path beside the hotel to complete her getaway, she had convinced herself that it really was too nice of a day to spend it inside working on the clutter still on the top of her desk. The wind out of the south ruffled her hair, and part of her bangs fell onto her face. She smiled to herself as she breathed in the pleasant fragrance of the narcissus that lined the border of the lawn that she was strolling. She began to think how different her life had become since she moved to this area and out of the stress of the Miami scene.

Her smile widened as she thought of her life back in Syracuse and how boring she had thought her existence was before she moved to Miami. With a university degree in hotel management, a divorce behind her, and an itch to get away, KaSandra decided she'd try Miami instead of New York City. Most of her friends had moved to the Big Apple to live and work, but she really wanted to be out of the state but still stay on the East Coast.

With a few years of experience in Miami behind her, she found working for a hotel that wanted long hours and low salary for their employees most deadly. Living back home in Syracuse would have been at least good for her health and attitude. As she reached the end of the path that led to the hotel, she remembered that she had not told her backup, Judith, that she was leaving, so she retraced her steps to the back of the bar area.

Judith Polymer stood by the bar's cash register daydreaming as she watched the waves hit the beach where a small child was building a sandcastle. As KaSandra approached the bar, Judith smiled and said in an approaching but still a playful manner, "I was wondering if I was going to be told where you were off to and how long you would be gone."

KaSandra answered jokingly, "If I tell you my every move, we'd never get any work done. I thought I'd take the rest of the day off. I just don't seem to be able to concentrate on what needs to be done, and I seem to be my own worst enemy today."

"Sounds like a good idea to me. Will you be back in time for dinner here, or should I tell Joe not to expect you?" Joe Flowers was the hotel's excellent chef, and no one wanted to miss any of his creations if they could help it.

"No," KaSandra answered as she started to walk away. "No need bothering to mention it for I'll be back in time for dinner."

Judith smiled to herself as she watched KaSandra walk down the beach toward the public sidewalk that led up to the street and out of her sight. Judith knew from experience as the hotel's bar manager that as long as KaSandra was away, she was in charge. This had been her third time being head bartender/manager of a bar area in seven years but the first time that anyone trusted her enough to just up and leave her in charge like KaSandra did every so often. Judith liked the feeling.

Judith stood about five six with short black hair tight to her head; her strong wiry body and pretty face with sparkling brown eyes threw everyone off when they first met her and most patrons of the hotel and bar knew that she could deal with any customer who got out of line. Judith found that reasoning with most of the clientele worked best without the help of force.

Thanks to her father's insistence that she take self-defense classes many years before, Judith found that force was not needed. Mostly, outmaneuvering her opponent gave her the advantage. She fell in love with the power, strength, and success she had after getting that black belt. There was also her background of living on the streets of Harlem with her six brothers and three sisters that gave her a leverage that most people did not expect.

Leaving the streets of Harlem many years before, Judith ended up in the Keys with just enough money for a bowl of soup and maybe some coffee. After getting into a few scrapes with the law, she needed a place to rest before starting again. Stopping at the bar in the Spanish Piece Duo that first night, Judith sat down and asked for a glass of water before inquiring about a job.

To her good fortune, Jac was in town and sitting at the far end of the bar when Judith entered, and he overheard her asked about work. Looking up, Jac liked what he saw and asked, "What can you do? And when did you eat last?"

Judith, used to males hitting on her, was about to tell the tall stranger to mind his own business but stopped as her brain registered, and she heard him say in the same breath, "When did you eat last?"

Looking up at the bartender, she asked in a low voice, "Who is he?"

The bartender, whose name was Peter, smiled and said, "He's the boss."

That had been almost one and a half years since Jac had given her the job as the hotel's bar manager and rescued her from a life most likely to be on the streets.

Judith lost track of time as the bar started to get busy and hadn't noticed that Kassandra's accustomed hour to return and eat had come and gone. As the dusk turned to dark Judith began to get worried about KaSandra's tardiness. She knew KaSandra could take care of herself, but it was not like her to not call if she was going to be delayed for any reason.

CHAPTER 3

Jac had just left the courthouse in Washington D.C., where he had testified in a case in which his client's ex-husband, Abdul Al-Harbi, was convicted of transporting their child across state lines and attempting to leave the country without custodial parent's permission. The child's mother, Ruth Anderson Al-Harbi, a citizen of the U.S., had hired him at his Washington D.C. office/home to find and get her son back after his father did not return the boy on time, afraid that her ex-husband had the idea of leaving the country. Jac had learned, after some investigation and the help of the FBI Department in Washington D.C., that the ex-spouse had purchased a passport for himself and a child several months ago. Now the D.C. Police Department said that on his usual customary weekend with his son, he had not returned him. Checking further, he had learned from one of his female friends in the airlines that his client's ex-husband had purchased two tickets for Paris and ending in Saudi Arabia, which leaving at seven p.m. the next night on Continental Air out of New York's La Guardia Airport.

Jac quickly alerted the customs departments, the NPD, and the FBI to be on the lookout for a dark-looking man of Middle Eastern description and traveling with a small boy. He was not the custodial parent according to the divorce papers and had not returned the boy after his customary weekend visit. It was thought that the lad was most likely going to be removed from the country illegally and must be stopped. Given the passport number Jac had obtained from his friend in the FBI, he finally felt that the pieces were starting to fall into place. The night following the alert, the authorities spotted the man and child trying to board the Continental plane. The child was put into protective custody and the father into cuffs.

His client's smiling face the day after her son was retrieved from his father was the last sight he saw as he left for his residence in D.C. via a helicopter ride; in that city, his job was finished. He would soon be returning to his hotel in the Keys, but first, he would spend a few days relaxing by his pool at his penthouse. He was still thinking of the conversation he had with Judith the other night as he pulled into the garage of the hotel where he resided when not in the Keys. He honked and waved at Jim Nelson, the garage attendant, before pulling into his parking spot.

Judith returned the menu to the table without ordering anything for breakfast. Seeing Judith frown and hearing her say that she didn't have an appetite that morning put many questions into Joe's mind as he carried toast, honey, orange juice, and a cup of coffee for Judith.

"Judith, when is the boss due in?"

"Oh, not until one o'clock or so. He is catching the noon flight out of Washington," she stated, sipping the coffee as she stared off into space.

Joe could tell from her expression that he wasn't going to get any more out of her right now, and he had many guests that would soon want to be fed. He headed toward the kitchen, turning when he heard the receptionist tell Judith that there was a Mike O'Hara on the phone for her. This information made him stop in his tracks and ask, "What do you want with that private detective?"

Judith ignored Joe as she reached for the phone to talk to Mike. She thought about how she was going to explain the situation to get Mike to act without sounding too concerned. Even though she was concerned by this time, especially after all the nightmares she had about KaSandra last night. Reaching for the receiver, she said, "Hi Mike."

The deep baritone of the retired police officer turned private investigator was very relaxing to Judith as he repeated her "Hi" and asked, "What's up Judy, and how is everyone at the hotel? It's been a long time since I heard from anyone over there, especially that Jac. Where is he anyway?" Judith laughed. "The same old Mike. How many times do I have to tell you my name is Judith, and Jac's fine. He should be in here from D.C. about one this afternoon. Say, I was wondering if you could come over here sometime after one so we can talk."

"Sure, sweetie. What's up?"

"Not now if that is alright, Mike."

"Sounds mysterious, just up my alley. I'll be there. How about two o'clock? That should give old Jac plenty of time to get from the airport."

Judith laughed again. "That will be fine for Jac would probably want to be here."

"Okay. Are you sure you can't give me a little hint? It will drive me crazy until two."

"No, I would rather not over the phone," Judith replied.

"Okay. See you then." Mike hung up.

Judith wished that she had said something, but she was still unsure that the whole situation was not just in her head. KaSandra was probably safe and would just walk through the front door any minute.

CHAPTER 4

Ten minutes after one o'clock, on the sixteenth of February, through the front door of his hotel, in walks Jac Scarin. Being away for several weeks, it was good to be back. After placing his suitcase by the reception desk, he greets the receptionist, Crystal, by her first name.

"Hi, Crystal, isn't it a wonderful day?"

His greeting reacted on Crystal the same way it did with most women of her age and demeanor. Seeing Jac sent hot flashes down her body, and the thought *if only* came to her mind every time.

Jac was 5"11½' and one hundred eighty-five pounds soaking wet. He had very square shoulders that moved down to a waist that most men would die for. He still looked and moved like he was a cat burglar moving in on his treasure despite his age. At forty-five, Jac, with his black haircut in an Italian style and turning a little gray at the temples, most people would guess he's about five years younger. His skin always looked tan and had a sheen to it that glowed of health. His sky blue eyes that twinkled every time he smiled would give you the idea that he knows something about you, and that thought just came to Crystal again upon his approach.

As Jac reached the front desk, he noticed that Crystal had a new dress on. At least he had not seen it before, and he usually notices that kind of item on the women that worked for him.

"Crystal, where is Judith?" he asked.

"Oh! Hi, Mr. Scarin. Welcome back."

"Crystal," Jac said, putting up his hand, "we are family here and—"

"Oh yes, sorry...Jac. I believe Judith is in the bar."

"Thanks, and is that a new dress?" Jac asked as he turned to walk toward the bar area in the back. Taking a few steps, he stopped on the spot and looked over his shoulder to see Crystal smiling to herself, happy that someone noticed that she had a new dress on.

"Well," he said with the sound of laughter in his voice, making her jump for she had thought he had left. She turned a slight pink as she nodded her head in an answer, too self-conscious to say anything. Jac, seeing this, laughed then said, "It looks great on you." Winking, he walked toward the bar.

As Jac took the curve around the bar area, he noticed Mike O'Hara coming in from the beach. Smiling, he offered his hand as Mike shook the sand off his shoes and reached for Jac's open palm.

"Well, what's the great mystery that got me to run over? Judy wouldn't tell me anything over the phone."

"Well, Mike, Judith phoned me in New York and thinks something has happen to

KaSandra, but I think we better let Judith fill us in. She's over there. Why don't we join her?"

Both men crossed the patio where Judith sat, trying to concentrate on ordering supplies for the bar and organizing the bills for the accountant to pay. As they reached her, she was about to pour herself another cup of coffee. Looking up, she smiled at both of them walking toward her.

Judith started to study both the men as they walked across from the beach entrance. *How had these two men gotten together?* she wondered to herself. Jac was tall, slender, and handsome, while Mike was a squat man built like a square block, not really fat but solid looking. *He must be at least fifteen years older than Jac with that gray hair that look like a lion's main, an ex-police on top of it. Well, he's not too bad for an ex-policeman.* Judith had never gotten along with the police, but she kind of like this person just the way he is, rough around the edges.

"Coffee?"

Mike said, "Yes, please."

"No, I would prefer a Fresca," said Jac.

Judith asked Peter, who was tending the bar, to bring one cup of coffee and a Fresca and then turned her attention to the two men who were joining her.

"Well, Judy—ah, Judith, what's the big mystery?"

"Oh, how to start," said Judith.

Jac, seeing how nervous she is, pats her hand that was resting next to her coffee cup, saying, "Have you heard from KaSandra since last night?"

"No, not a word."

"Wait just a minute here. Back up. Where is KaSandra?" said Mike.

"That is the whole mystery Mike," said Judith trying to stay calm. "I do not know. She left here around noon yesterday and said she would be back in time for dinner, and we have not heard from her since."

"Oh well. Does she have a new romance that she gotten involved with and just forgot to call?" asked Mike with a smile.

"Not that I know of, and even if she did, she would not forget to call. She is just too meticulous."

"Judith, was she in any kind of mood or on medication?" asked Mike.

Before Judith could answer, Peter comes over to the table with a tray, and hearing Mike's question, he said, "KaSandra, wouldn't ever take anything stronger than aspirin. She lost an older brother to drugs, and that loss nearly killed her." Setting Jac's glass down a little too arduously, Peter splatters the liquid into the table.

"Easy, Pete, Mike is just trying to get a handle on the facts," said Judith.

Jac frowned as he heard this news about KaSandra. He didn't know that she had lost her brother, let alone having him overdose on drugs.

"Thanks, Pete, I know how worried you are about her, and I am sure Mike will find KaSandra's whereabout very soon," said Judith.

Smiling at Judith, Peter turned and walked back to the bar.

"Boy, is everyone that wired?" asked Mike. "Tell me all you can about KaSandra and how you perceived her yesterday, Judith, so that I can have a place to start."

"Let me see." Judith started to think and talk out load. "I think she looked a little tired, and as I told Jac over the phone last night, a little absentminded the past two weeks. She has put in lots of hours getting everything ready for the opening of the International Bankers Conference. I think that was why she decided to take the afternoon off yesterday. She must have been aware that she was snapping at everyone recently and never completed her sentences."

"Would there be a certain place that she would go to unwind if she wanted to be alone other than her rooms here?" questioned Mike.

Judith nodded and said, "She would probably go to one of the beaches on the other side of the Keys, but which one, I would not know."

"Now were getting somewhere. What did she have on?"

Judith sighed, and after thinking a minute, shook her head and said, "I really do not remember. I had been concentrating on my paperwork and can just remember that she said she was going out for the rest of the afternoon. I bet that Crystal would remember though."

Jac, who had sat with his back to the bar, turned toward it and asked, "Pete, would you please ring Crystal and ask her to come back to the patio for a few minutes? Oh, and tell her to put the phones on forward out here."

As Pete nodded and picked up the phone, Jac turned back to the table and spoke to Mike. "Mike, what does your instincts tell you about the situation with KaSandra?"

"With what I know about KaSandra since she started at the hotel, I think what Judith has said is probably true. That she wouldn't just go off for an extended time and not tell someone." He turned to Judith and asked, "Judith, do you have a recent picture of KaSandra that I can have for a few days?"

"Yes. I thought you might ask for one, so I brought this one down from my apartment." Here is a photo of the two of us on the beach. I took it a month ago." She handed the picture across to Mike just as Crystal walked up and sat down on the empty chair next to her.

Jac smiled at Crystal again and proceeded to ask if she remembered what KaSandra had on the day when she left.

Crystal was a heavy set woman who was semi-retired and only worked three days a week. Crystal said in her Mississippi accent, "Why, yes, she had on her lime green long skirt and matching top. Oh, and a scarf with matching sandals and shoulder bag all in red. She always looks so good in that outfit. Mr. Jac, do you know where she is? If she doesn't get back here pretty soon, the whole hotel is going to fall apart, and the big banking conference is coming up in a few days."

"No, Crystal, that's why Mike is here," said Jac.

"We're going to do a little looking around and see if we can come up with what, if anything, happened to her." She nodded her head when the phone rang. Pete picked it up and said it was for Crystal. She rose from the chair and walked to the bar in a way you would think her feet were hurting.

"I guess I better get started. First, I'll get some copies made of this photo, then hit the north side of the Keys's beach area," said Mike.

As Mike rose from the chair, Jac said, "I'll walk you out, Mike. There is still something else I want to discuss with you."

As everyone left, Judith tried to get back to the stack of papers in front of her but found it hard to concentrate. Catching herself wandering and staring out at the ocean, she thought, *why not swim to get the kinks out and relieve some of this tension.* With that, she rose from the table and walked to the stairs that led up to her room on the first floor.

CHAPTER 5

After making a dozen or so photos, O'Hara started up to the north shore beaches to begin the legwork of looking for some more clues on KaSandra's disappearance.

As he drove, he thought back to the first day he had met KaSandra. She had just started work at the hotel, and his first opinion of her was a quiet but a very beautiful female. She seemed all business until you caught her interest in what you were saying, and then it was like someone turned on a lamp, and she would light up in so many different ways, not enough, though, to let people know of her troubles, especially about her brother. By the expression on his face when Peter came out with that news, it was sure that Jac didn't know.

Wow!

The traffic was not as heavy as the usual for this time of the year. This was the time when tourists came down to avoid the winter months in the north. It was probably the clouds that kept them off the coastal road, which he took to get to the northern beaches. The rain started to come, so Mike reached for the windshield wipers; this made him think about how bad it would be if KaSandra were out in this downpour.

The rain had made the drive to the other side of the island a little slower than usual. Soon, he spotted his first stop, Sea and Shells, where he had decided to show KaSandra's photograph and maybe leave a few for the owner to put up. Sea and Shells was a shop where tourists could get souvenirs, food, and drinks all in one stop as stated on the sign on the door. The shop was a good business for the owner whom Mike had known for at least a decade. Mike stepped through the door of Sea and Shells and spotted the owner, whose name was Guy Peterson, behind the counter. Just as Mike was about to call out, Guy hailed him. "My stars! What in the hell brings a scrubby PI like you up here? Pleasure, I hope?"

"No, Guy. I only wish. I'm on a hunt for someone and thought that maybe you might have seen her." Mike took a seat at the bar and pulled out the photo of KaSandra; he handed it over to Guy who was just finishing the glasses that were in the sink. Guy, wiping his hands on a towel that was around his waist and scooping up the photo, said, "Wow, she's a beauty. Is she wanted for something?"

"No," said Mike, "she's a friend who's been missing from her position at the Spanish Piece Duo for almost two days now."

"Yes, of course! I've seen her face before. The little lady and me had stayed at that hotel when we were on the south side. Sorry, Mike, I haven't seen her since that time. How about a drink for the road?"

"No thanks, Guy, it's a little early for me, and I've got a lot of places on this side of the Keys to stop at before dark. See you later!"

As Mike walked back out into the rain, he wondered how hard this was going to be. The next stop was at a friend of Jac's, who he said was part of the family. *I wonder how many friends of Jac's are down here in the Keys from his old neighborhood. I sure like Jac, but some of the people I've met over the years that are his so-called friends I'd really stay clear of.*

As Mike drove further up the coast, he started his search for the street numbers for Jac had told him that this Anthony Costello was just off Big Torch Key, at Post Box 2004. Also, Jac had said that he would give Tony a call and make sure he was available for a visitor. *Available boy.* "I wonder who this guy is," he said out loud just as he drove past 2004 on the left side of the road.

CHAPTER 6

Anthony Castillo had come from a mixed family heritage; he was born of an Italian mother and an Irish father. His father, Patrick, had come to the U.S. after an English soldier in Northern Ireland killed both his parents during a demonstration. Anthony's father struggled for ten years, trying to make a living in a city where Irish men were not wanted. One day, after selling his pile of newspapers to the wealthier people of New York, Patrick came upon a group of three thugs beating a young guy as he was heading back to his sublet room. Seeing how outnumbered the young man was and always in the mood for a good fight, he joined in, and the number soon dwindled. Patrick Castillo offered his hand to his combative partner and pulled him to his feet as the last hooligan hit the ground.

"Hi, I Patrick Castillo, and are you all right, chum?"

Salazar Scarin shook his head as he held his handkerchief up to his nose to stop the blood.

"What were they beating you up for anyway?" Patrick asked.

Salazar found his voice and said, "I'm Salazar Scarin, and I would not pay up for their protection and got several others in my block's businesses to refuse too. They decided to make an example out of me. Do you realize that your aid to me has put you in danger? They are against the Irish just as strongly as they are out for the Italians."

"Oh sure, but I can't keep my nose out of a good fight, especially when the numbers are all on one side."

Salazar started to laugh and cough at the same time, saying, "You have a real nice left hook there and are quick on your feet for such a scrawny guy. How tall are you anyway?"

"Oh, five eleven or so, and as you already have stated, I'm Irish, and we learn to fight early in life to stay alive," Patrick replied.

"I hear you. So now that you got your exercise for the day," Salazar finally asked, "would you be interested in a good home-cooked Italian meal? I was on my way home when I ran into those goons, and even though my lip is cut and this eye is going to close if I don't get something on it, I'm still hungry."

"Sure, you bet. I haven't had a real home-cooked meal since my mother's, back in Ireland ten years ago."

Upon arrival at the Salazar's family home, both men were greeted with questions about their appearance, and they had to satisfy Mrs. Scarin's worried face. Patrick, with no family in the U. S., was quickly adopted by the Scarins and became the second son and brother to Salazar's four sisters. After being a constant visitor in the Scarin's family home for four years, Patrick married Salazar's sister Maria and became a permanent member of the Scarin's clan. He joined Salazar in the family's brokerage business, which sold commodities, and started raising his own family, and that included Anthony, who is also called Tony.

Patrick Castillo, at the early age of fourteen, had joined the rackets of the '20s and '30s in the City of New York as a runner and ended up in the juvenile detention system more than he was out. His periods of freedom brought him in contact with Tony's mother, Maria, who was a member of the next generation of Scarin women. He married her while he was still a whiskey bootlegger for the big bosses and while he was still making a good living for himself. Because of the nature of his work, Patrick knew that his life could end at any time and decided to raise his children in the finest style that money could provide, including the best schools. His belief was that a good education would keep them out of the rackets and into proper society. After Tony's birth, Patrick Castillo tried his best to stay within the law and out of prison. One night, while working late at the factory that still dealt in illegal whiskey, he was shot through the head gangland style.

This left Tony to be the head of the family, and just about to finish Harvard Law school, Tony decided to stay with the practice of law and continue working with his family, but not always the way his rich friends considered righteous. This made life very interesting for Tony, even if it turned out to be not always completely legal for the Scarin part of his family still thrived on the seamier part of life and often needed his help to beat the system.

Jac Scarin, Tony's nephew, decided to take a joyride with his two female cousins and a couple other boys in a brand new "borrowed" Cadillac after his sixteenth birthday party. Jac, a new and inexperience driver, found that the car was too great a challenge for the rainy afternoon that he and his accomplices confiscated it. Coming down the coastal highway a little too fast found them over the hill and into the Atlantic Ocean. All bailed out of the car just as it entered the water and sunk out of sight. Jac's father, upon hearing about the incident from the police, was ready to let the thieves, including his son and his cousins, rot in the county jail. Uncle Tony realized that this would cause future trouble and negotiated the owner to drop the charges against the culprits for a sizable amount of compensation and a new car. Tony later got Jac to agree that at some future date, when he requested payment, Jac would pay without questions. Jac agreed wholeheartedly to stay out of jail.

CHAPTER 7

Turning the car around, Mike drove back to where he saw the 2004 number and pulled up to the gate—a six-foot-tall gate connected to a fence that was at the same height and seemed to go on for blocks. Mike was not expecting an estate when Jac said that the relative lived up on the coast. Rolling down his window, he pushed the security system button and waited for an answer.

There came a voice, immediately asking, "Yes, whom would you like to see?"

Mike asked for Anthony Castillo and added, "Jac Scarin has made an appointment for me to talk with Mr. Castillo."

"Yes, he's been waiting for you, Mr. O'Hara. Won't you drive right up to the front door park, and someone will meet you there."

The box went silent, and the gate started to swing open. Mike drove up the long driveway and parked just to the side of the horseshoe circle. Mike got out of the car and noticed a fashionable woman in a beige suit that stood watching him from the top step of the patio, which led into the rather exclusive mansion.

"Hello, Mr. O'Hara, I'm Mr. Castillo's private secretary. Won't you come inside?"

Mike nodded and followed the attractive young woman across the patio and through huge Ziricote wood doors that led into a black-and-white tiled entrance hall. The secretary asked him to wait there just a moment and disappeared through the double doors on the left side of the hall, which she closed as she went. Mike looked around and noticed that there were double doors on the other side of this rather large entry hall. At the far end of the room was a writing desk in mahogany with a marble top and matching mahogany antique straight-backed chair. The room was void of any appearance of being lived in except the staircase that led to the second floor, which is also in Ziricote.

After what seemed to be only a few minutes, the secretary reappeared and said, "Mr. O'Hara, would you follow me? Mr. Castillo will see you now."

"Sure!" Mike walked across the floor and entered a large room that was papered in a creamy color, the same as the entrance hallway. There was expensive furniture, a fireplace, and two more double doors that led out to a patio on the other side of the room.

As the secretary closed the door, Mike asked, "What do they call you anyway?"

She looked his way, smiled, and said, "I'm called Ms. Bermo," and then she turned and led the way through the far doors to the patio.

On the veranda, Mike saw what looked like expensive rattan furniture. Four slightly curved chairs of different sizes covered in a pale tan, six deck chairs spread out against the sides of the patio, and a round table covered with a silver tea set, china cups, and saucers enough for four people.

In one of the four chairs that had a rather tall back set sat a stylish older man in a pair of cream-colored slacks belted at a slim waist, a brown Polo pullover opened at the neck, and dark brown loafers. He also had a well-muscled body, square shoulder, and a windswept look to his face, which showed every line. On the top of his head, there was some very thick white hair. Mike's environment took the man's appearance in quickly as Anthony Castillo turned with the introduction that came from Ms. Bermo.

"Mr. Castillo, Mr. O'Hara is here to see you."

Getting out of the chair with a friendly smile, Tony Castillo stretched out his hand and said, "Hi Mike."

"Mr. Castillo," Mike repeated his name as he shook the amazingly strong hand.

"No, please call me Tony. All my friends do and any friend of Jac's is, I hope, a friend of mine. What can I do for you?"

Mike smiled and said, "Did Jac tell you anything about what we are doing?"

"Yes, he filled me in a little."

Tony turned toward the table and Ms. Bermo, who stood quietly, "Would you like some coffee, tea, or something stronger to heat the bones now that this storm has passed by?"

"Yes, thanks. I'll take a cup of hot tea and lemon, if you have it."

"Are you sure on that tea, Mike? I have scotch and soda, and I understand it is your pleasure," said Tony with a smile.

"Well, maybe a light one with a splash of soda," Jac must have squealed.

Tony laughed and asked Ms. Bermo if she would do the honors before she left for her break. Turning back to Mike, he said, "Let's go over here on this side of the deck in the sun and have our chat."

Leading the way, Tony asked, "How is Jac? I have not seen him in. It must be three months now, and then out of the blue, he calls and asks for a favor. Here, we live less than a half hour from each other, and he can't come and see me."

"How long have you known Jac?" Mike asked even though he probably knew already, but he wanted to change the subject.

"Oh, our families have been connected to each other for generations, way back to my grandfather about fifty years. The two families have been intermarrying since my grandfather helped Jac's grandfather out of a fight and end up marrying his sister Maria Scarin. I guess you could call me his uncle or something like that."

Just then, Ms. Bermo walked over and placed the drinks on a small table that was between the two chairs. "Martha," said Mr.

Castillo, "You might as well go on your break now. I'll probably not need you for at least an hour."

"Very well, Mr. Castillo," and she turned and walked a few steps, stopped, then turned around and stated, "I will be leaving the grounds. Is there anything you need that I can pick up?" Tony Castillo shook his head in reply, and Martha left the patio.

"Pretty woman," Mike said.

"Yes," said Tony. "Her father is my partner in some of my business ventures. After I lost my last secretary, I thought of her and ask her to join me. I don't always like to talk in front of her though, for personal reasons. There are some things that I would not like her to know and speak of to her father." Tony's voice trailed off as if he was thinking of some particular business.

"Now, on to the business that you are here for," said Tony.

"I don't know how much Jac filled you in on, but one of our friends, and she's also the manager of his hotel, has disappeared," stated Mike. "We have assessed that she loves the beaches on this side of the Keys when she wants to think, and we figured that is where she was coming on her afternoon off two days ago."

Tony held up his hand to stop Mike's story. "Wait, why are you so concerned after only two days?"

Mike nodded. "Yes, I know that is a short time for anyone to be gone, but you have to know KaSandra and that Jac is interested in her welfare. Besides, she is a very meticulous person who always does what she says she going to do.

"I've been told by the people at the hotel that she said she'd be back at six o'clock two days ago for dinner and never showed. She also didn't make any calls to state her change of mind or plans. All Jac had in mind, Tony, I'm sure, was for you to keep the eyes and ears of your contacts on this end of the Keys open for news of her. We don't want to interfere with her personal business. I'm just trying to find her and make sure she's all right. I can leave you a few of these pictures in case you hear of a woman answering her description, then if you do hear anything, you can let Jac or I know."

Tony put up his hand again to stop Mike. "Mike, I can do better than that. I will make a few inquires while you're still here and see if anyone has any news of her. Why don't you have another drink and help yourself to a little light lunch that my staff has just set up. I will be back as fast as I can with what news I can find out."

"Gee thanks. I am a little hungry," said Mike as Tony crossed the veranda and entered the house. While Mike waited for Tony to return, he helped himself to another scotch and soda, picked up a plate from the end of the table, and filled it with all sorts of delicious-looking food.

There was all kind of meats, which included lean roast beef, his favorite. For the fish lover, he noted some shrimp and crab and in two silver containers, some rice and mashed potatoes with gravy. That looked delicious. On the side, there was a big crystal bowl filled with crisp lettuces and various garnishes and dressings for your pleasure all marked with their names.

At the far end of the table were several deserts, which looked very fattening, a silver coffee urn and teapot with cups and saucers.

Mike helped himself to several pieces of roast beef, some mashed potatoes with gravy, a wheat dinner roll with butter, and a few of the garnishes. With a filled plate, a mug, and silverware in hand, Mike walked back to where they had been sitting and dug in to the delicious food.

Just as Mike was about to finish the last bite of apple pie that was in front of him, Tony walked back onto the veranda. Tony stopped at the table and picked up a cup and saucer and the coffeepot. Then he walked over to Mike, sat down, poured himself a cup of coffee, and refilled Mike's mug.

"Mike, I've talked to some of my sources, and at this point, they have not seen Ms. Martin, but I have left instruction to keep looking and report back to me if she is found."

"I also put a call into a Dr. Frederick Calendar, who runs a small clinic on this end of the Keys. He may have heard something from his staff or patients. If she's hurt in anyway, someone might have taken her over there for aid." He was with a patient when I called and will return my call as soon as he is finished. That is about all I can do right now, but if I hear anything, I will contact Jac immediately."

Getting to his feet, he said, "You will have to excuse me for I have another appointment that I must keep, but Mike, do help yourself to more food and refreshments. It is nice to meet you." Tony walked around the table and down some steps on the left side of the patio. Upon reaching the grass, he took a path that led to the beach.

CHAPTER 8

As Mike walked toward the table of food, he thought that, that was a nice but abrupt dismissal. *I guess I'll show myself out right after I retrieve one more piece of the apple pie.* Mike got back into his car still licking is fingers after devouring the piece of pie that he removed from the table on his way out. He started the motor and dialed Jac's number at the same time. He wanted to update him about his talk with Tony Castillo.

The hotel's receptionist picked up on the first ring and relayed that Jac was out of the hotel but might be reached through his car phone.

"Thanks, Crystal. I've got that number, so I'll give it a try." As Mike wheeled down the driveway out of the Castillo Estate, the phone in Jac's car began to ring. Jac answered the ring, and before Mike could reply, Ms. Bermo, in her Porsche, drove through the gate and stopped directly in front of his exiting car.

"Hold on a minute, Jac. I'll be right back. There is a little business to attend to."

His instinct told him that she had stopped deliberately and the next move was his. Getting out of his car, he walked over to the driver's side of her car and asked, "Is there something I can do for you, Ms. Bermo?" He knew that his voice sounded sarcastic, but after all, she had started it by being very cold when they met.

"Yes, you can wipe that sneer off your face and ask me out."

"What makes you think I'm even interested, Ms. Bermo?"

39

"Come on now, Mr. Mike O'Hara, P.I., I saw how you watched me across the patio. Oh, and you know my first name, so why not use it?"

"Oh, really Martha, so you want to go out with me?"

"Yes, so why don't you pick me up at 6:30 back here at the estate?"

"All right, you've got a date. Now, do you mind moving your car so I can get out of here and finished the rest of my day's business?"

"I'll see you at 6:30," Martha said as he turned and walked back to the car and hoped that Jac was still holding on the other end of the phone.

While Jac was waiting for Mike's return, he started thinking about the car called Porsche and how distinct the sound was, how he could recognize the car by the hum of its motor. The very unique design and placement of the engine. The horizontally opposed six-cylinder setup is extremely efficient, which translates into a very clean sound. That deep nice rumble due to the exhaust setup of the engine in the back. Then his mind returned to Mike just as Mike picked up the phone again and drove out the estate's gate. He could hear Jac's laughter on the other end of the line. "Hey, Mike, what's her name? Was that a Porsche motor that I heard, and are you still at Tony's estate?" Jac said.

Mike laughed back into the phone and answered by saying, "Yes to the last two questions, and her name is Martha Bermo."

"Martha, watch out for that one. She is hot and looking for a husband the last time I saw her," said Jac.

"Yeah thanks, but that's not why I buzzed you. I'm just leaving the estate and thought I'd bring you up to date." He paused. "Mr. Castillo was very pleasant and hopefully helpful, if some of his contacts come up with something," said Mike. "He did mention a Dr. Frederick Calendar. I thought I'd have a friend at the police department check it out. Unless you know of him for he's new to me."

"Yes, I have heard of him. He came to the Keys about two years ago, from Germany I believe. He started a clinic for the research into reproduction and stays mostly to himself, seeing only his patients."

"What kind of clientele does he have?" asked Mike.

"Oh, I believe the very wealthy couples that cannot get a family started and need some kind of outside help reproducing. Mike, it would not hurt to have your buddy check him out though, but why did Tony call him?"

"Oh, he being a doctor. Anyone finding an injured person might take them to see Calendar, Tony figured."

"Did he get any answer?" asked Jac

"Tony said the doctor was with a patient and would get back to him when he's finished. Then Tony will give you a call. Oh, by the way, Tony is not very happy with you and said you haven't been up to see him. He said he was your uncle on the other side of the family."

"Well, Mike, he's my uncle, godfather, and my mother's brother. I owe him quite a lot for some help he did for me and the family some years back…" said Jac.

"Say, you're breaking up. You must be getting out of range. I'll talk to you later," said Mike and hung up the car phone. He made a call to his friend at the police station and then pulled into a gas station for some more fuel and a pit stop.

CHAPTER 9

When Jac got the call from Mike, he was on his way to the Ramrod Keys. As Jac thought about KaSandra and the conversations they usually have late in the evenings when everything was quiet, it came back to him that she had mentioned Ramrod Key as a wonderful area to explore. It had a lot of interesting little sections of beaches that hardly anyone visited. If she wanted some peace and quiet and a chance to think, Judith stated maybe that is where she had gone. As he steered his convertible off Route 1 and on to the beach road, he saw the northern route bus parked in the wayside rest area. On a hunch, he parked his car and crossed the field that spanned the area between the beach and the rest area. Reaching the bus, he showed the driver Kass's photo and asked him if he remembered seeing KaSandra on the bus that afternoon three days ago. Taking a photo that Jac was handing him, the driver said he had driven the route on that day and that she sure looked familiar.

"Good, but did you see her three days ago on the bus?" asked Jac, trying to keep his voice calm.

"That's just what I said, man. She got on in front of that hotel, on the other side, and rode all the way up here to this rest stop."

"Yes, what did she do then?" Jac asked, holding a ten-dollar bill in his hand.

"The same thing she always does. She takes off her dress, down to her bathing suit, and walked down that path over there." The driver was pointing to a path that led down to the beach.

Jac asked, "Do you happen to know how she gets back to the other side when she comes out here?"

"Sure, she catches my bus usually two or three hours later."

"Can you remember if she caught your bus, going back to the other side that day after you left her off here?" Jac asked.

"No man, I don't remember seeing her again now that you ask," said the driver, taking the bill from Jac's hand and stuffing it in his shirt.

"Well, thanks for the information," Jac said. He turned, walked back to his car, and drove down the rest of the way to the beach before parking and walking south along the water. He did not really know what he was looking for but thought he had to do something to help solve the mystery of KaSandra's disappearance. As he walked, he could see why she liked this part of the north shore. It was really beautiful and peaceful. He had walked about a mile when he figured and decided to turn around and retrace his steps back to the car. After eating the lunch made for him by the hotel's kitchen, he walked north along the shore in hopes of finding something. He walked until the sun was almost down and decided that it would soon be too late to see anything. He started back toward the car when he noticed something red amongst the rocks. Bending to retrieve the article, he noticed it was a piece of red scarf, which had several holes, as if someone had torn it off. Remembering what Crystal had said about KaSandra wearing red accessories— scarf, handbag, and shoes—he started to think that maybe this was the spot were KaSandra had set up her beach chair. Her exclusive spot was perfect—not much wave action and not many visitors. *Anything could happen here. I'll have to talk to her about safety when she gets back.* Looking further, he found many sandal footsteps in the surrounding area. He could not be certain that any were hers or if she had been joined by anyone else. He decided the best move was to hurry back to the car and call Mike for some help. This had been the first clue anyone had, had in three days. They needed to start searching this beach and area for more clues. There was no answer on Mike's car phone, so he decided to return to the hotel and get some help from the employees and maybe a search dog to help. As Jac entered the hotel, the receptionist called out to him and said, "Mr. Castillo called for him several times, and he sounds most urgent. He would call again at 8:30 p.m." Jac checked his watch and saw that it was 8:25 p.m., so he asked the night receptionist to put the call through to his suite as soon as it came through. Turning, he went straight to the stairs, took two at a time to the first floor, and walked straight to his suite.

He was just pulling a clean turtleneck over his head when the phone rang. Reaching for the phone, he said, "Hello, is that you, Tony?"

"Uh, Jac, where the hell have you been? I got a call back from Dr. Calendar, and he said that there is a Jane Doe at his clinic that answers the description I gave him of KaSandra. He said that she been there for three days with amnesia and no identification, so they couldn't contact anyone."

"What not even the police? Tony, where do I find this Calendar," asked Jac, his voice showing the urgency of getting the information.

"He's up near Ramrod Keys on this side. What's up, Jac? Your voice tells me you got something."

"Tony how do you know this doctor? Does he live at the clinic, and if not, could you get him to meet us over there in about an hour? Do you know what kind of a license he has and whom he deals with?" said Jac.

"Hey, Jac, slow down. This is not like you," said Tony. "Think, man, it's now almost nine o'clock, and by the time you get back to this side of the Keys, it will be closer to ten. I don't think any doctor would be willing to disturb a patient at his clinic at that time. Why don't you drive sanely over here and stay overnight as my guest. We can call and go over to the clinic the first thing in the morning together."

Listening to his voice, Jac's urgency seemed to decline, and by the time Tony had finished talking, Jac was calm again and could see the logic in his uncle's words.

"Okay, that sound good, and I do owe you a visit. I'll be there in about an hour." Hanging up the phone, Jac reached for his sky blue sports jacket on the bed and walked toward the door, thinking as he walked downstairs that he should stop at the bar and fill Judith in on what had happened. As he approached the bar area, he noticed that she was quite busy and decided to leave a message with the receptionist that she and Mike should meet him at Tony's estate in the morning.

CHAPTER 10

Jac parked in the parking bay and had not walked about eight feet toward Tony's house when someone grabbed him from behind and pulled his jacket down over his arms, pinning them. Jac had, had enough self-defense back in the old neighborhood to react with a quick jerk forward. But a right hook into a left cross to his jaw. He felt his knees buckle and the darkness come over him, shutting out the world.

When Jac gained consciousness, he was sitting in a semi-darkened room, and his arms tied behind the chair. Across the room, on a well-stuffed sofa, sat his godfather, drinking a brandy and reading a book in the room's only light. As Jac surveyed the room, he noticed that he was in Tony's private library/sitting room, located on the second floor off the master bedroom. How he got up there and why they had tied him up, he had no idea. Jac, trying to straighten up, let out a small groan that alerted Tony that his guest was finally awake.

Getting off the sofa, Tony walked over to the chair. Lifted his godson's face to him and said, "Well, it's about time you gained consciousness. Sorry about the reception and treatment you received. My man was a little too rough, but I figured if I didn't get you secured before our little talk, you would probably walk out before I could finish. So if you promise to stay and listen to what I have to say, I'll untie you and get you a brandy. Otherwise, I'll just leave you that way until I'm finished talking."

"This is a fine way to treat someone you are supposed to love," said Jac. "You aren't giving me much of a choice, but I know one thing, that if you release me, I'm not the only one that is going to be hurting."

"Jac. Jac. You do remember the promise you gave me back some twenty-five years ago. If I helped you out of the mess you were in that you'd owe me, right? Well, this is payback for that promise. So why not be reasonable and let me untie you so we can get on with our conversation?"

"Okay," said Jac. "Untie me and I'll listen." Tony, leaning against the chair that Jac sat in, started hitting the wood with his knocks, saying at the same time, "Jac, can I trust you?"

All Jac could hear was Tony's knocks on the wood right behind his ear. "Why are you knocking? I've said it three times. Don't you realize I can't get away? I'm tied up."

Slowly, Jac came to the realization that the knocking was not from behind his head, but there was someone really knocking at the door of his bedroom in Tony's house. Coming to a sitting position and holding his head, Jac said, "Yeah, I hear you. Come on in." The door opened slowly, and the housekeeper came in carrying a breakfast table filled with food.

"Oh, you did not have to do that," said Jac.

"Yes, she did," said Tony as he walked through the door after the housekeeper. "I told her to bring up a good breakfast for you after last night's session."

Tony looked around the room, and when his eyes filled on the bed, he frowned and told the housekeeper to fix Jac's bed before she left. Turning to Jac, who was by this time up and looking out the window, Tony said, "From the looks of this bed, you probably didn't sleep a whole lot. Jac, boy, you got to learn to relax."

Jac chose to ignore Tony. His head ached after the grilling on the same old subject—working for Tony. That he got well into the morning along with who knows how much brandy he had and was worrying about KaSandra. He did not need another session with his godfather.

"Jac, I know I was rough on you last night, but the way your life has been going since, well, you know, I get concerned about you, and I'm not the only one." With this news, Jac turned around and looked at him.

"Who else is in on what happened last night?" he asked.

Tony looked at him as if to say "Do you have to ask?"

"Jac, I was bound to get you out here sooner or later for our talk, and you know I'm right. I'm just sorry you didn't come without a crisis on your mind. Now come on over here and eat a good breakfast before we start out for the clinic. Oh, by the way, while you were still asleep, Judith called and said she and Mike would be here about ten." Tony had walked to the door and was closing it after the housekeeper as he finished the sentence. Jac had still not moved from the window. The feeling of being sixteen again had still not left him from last night. He watched as Tony closed the door and thought that the discussion that occurred last night was still not over, and he had barely held his own.

Tony just smiled and pointed to the breakfast table, waiting for him. "Come on, my boy. Don't make me pull rank. We're not going anywhere if you don't eat a substantial breakfast. Who knows when you last had a decent one."

Jac knew that he better comply, so he walked over to the table, and seeing two cups for coffee, he turned and asked, "Will you have coffee with me?"

Jac did not realize how hungry he was until after he started to eat. This was a regular feast for he was not use to eating in the morning. A Fresca and bagel would usually do him just fine. But today, he ate bacon and eggs with two pieces of toast, smeared with raspberry jam—his favorite—and half of a grapefruit. As he poured himself another cup of coffee, Jac looked to see if Tony needed any more. He found Tony was smiling at him, and after covering the top of his cup with his hand, he said, "Well, don't you feel better now? The way you dug into that food, I assume that my comment must be correct."

Jac settled back with his cup of coffee and started to feel a little more secure. Smiling, he said, "Yes, I guess I have been acting a little crazy and childish the past eight hours, and I better get finished here and dress for ten o'clock is fast approaching. Only wish I had thought of bring a change of clothes." Tony got up, placed his coffee cup on the table, and softly struck Jac on the cheek.

"Yes, I agree. Oh, after your shower and shave, why not check the closet?" he asked as he turned and left the room.

Jac showered and started to pull on what he wore last evening, then remembered what Tony had said about the closet. He opened the wardrobe against the wall and found fresh clothing. Proceeding over to the highboy, he found fresh underwear, a charcoal-gray T-shirt, and gray socks. Putting the gray slacks off a hanger and the sky blue-colored sports coat from last night, he left the room and walked down to the living room.

Tony was on the phone as he entered. Mike and Judith had arrived and had coffee already set in front of them. Judith looked fantastic in her tan linen two-piece suit with a cream eyelet blouse. A strand of gold-linked round beads was around her neck, and it finished her outfit. Mike, on the other hand, was Mike. He had on a white shirt with no tie, slacks in black, and boots. His jacket that was thrown over the chair looked like he had slept in it.

"Good morning, you two. Is Tony talking to the clinic?" asked Jac

Judith looked up and smiled at Jac as he entered the room and said, "Hi, boss. Yes, Tony called to make sure Dr. Calendar had arrived at the clinic so we'll have no trouble getting in to see this patient."

"I sure hope it is KaSandra." Just as Judith finished saying KaSandra's name, Tony hung up the phone and walked over to where everyone was gathering.

"Well, it's all set. Dr. Calendar will meet us at the front desk."

"The unknown patient is being told that there are going to be some visitors in about twenty minutes that might know her identity."

"Shall we go? I had the chauffeur bring my car around so we can all go in comfort."

As the car slowed to a stop in front of the clinic, Jac noticed that the buildings were in Spanish style of orange/red tile roofs and white walls that seem to go on for a block. The back structures sat right up against a cliff that over looked the ocean. All along the highway, which drove along the cliffs, was a five-feet-tall wire fencing with shrubbery in front of them. For concealment, Jac wandered. The walls connected with a very ornate gate and guard station. As the party reached the front door, Jac also noticed that the front door, which was Ziricote, had the same design on it as the front gate, with a big *CC* engraved on a half moon.

As they entered the door, they were greeted immediately by the doctor. He was about five foot eight, black hair streaked with white, and a mustache that showed signs of turning white. He was dressed impeccably with a white linen suit, a white silk shirt, and a gray silk tie that had a faint red thread running through it and is pinned down with a diamond stud. A little of his gray slacks showed his loafers cut in the French style. A white lab coat worn open as a cover-up was also a very rich-looking linen.

It was his eyes that caught Jac's attention and instinctively put him on his guard. They were rather small in shape and so deep brown that they look black. It was the way that they looked at you even when the rest of his face was smiling. The eyes showed no hint of that smile but caught your attention, as if they were looking right through you.

Tony stepped forward and introduced himself as he shook the doctor's hand. "Dr. Calendar, I am Anthony Castillo. I believe that we already met at the fundraiser after the flooding of the Keys a few months ago."

"Yes, I remember you now," said Frederick.

After the doctor's greeting, Tony turned to Judith and stated, "Doctor, may I introduce some of my friends in search of their friend. This is Judith Polymer, Mike O'Hara, and Jac Scarin, we are all hoping that your mystery guest is a KaSandra Martin."

Frederick shook Judith's hand, covering it with both of his, and in doing so, he thought, "Boy, I wish I could get you into my clinic for a stay." Then he shook Mike and Jac's hand and stated, "Well, if you all come this way, I have Jane Doe in the visitor room, and she is quite excited to meet all of you," said Frederick as he showed them the way.

"Doctor," Jac stopped him from entering the area and asked, "is she still without her memory?"

"No, Mr. Scarin, she remembers everything that happened to her since she woke up here three days ago. It is just the day in question and her name that she does not seem to recall. I do not think it's permanent, and she should recover those memories also. Shall we go in?"

"One more thing, doctor, how did she get here? Can you tell us?" asked Jac.

"Certainly, I was out jogging on the beach that morning and found her unconscious next to a boulder. I presumed that she had fallen off the rock while climbing it. I looked around for someone else or some beach equipment—you know, a towel, umbrella, clothes bag, or purse—and found nothing. I quickly picked her up and carried her to my car after checking to see if she had anything broken. All I saw at the time were lots of minor bruises, but she must have hit her head, not to remember her fall. The moss and growth around the boulder must have softened the fall. So she was not seriously injured." The doctor, still holding the doorknob, turned and opened the door slowly, and smiled at a young woman sitting next to the window, reading a magazine.

"Jane, these are the people that I spoke to you about," said Dr. Calendar. Jane looked up and spied Jac right away.

As KaSandra's hand went to her face, they heard a small cry, and tears sprung to her eyes. She uttered the word *Jac*. A surprised look covered Jac's face, and his legs began to move toward the couch that KaSandra was sitting on. By the time Jac reached her, she was crying quite hard in relief. Jac knelt and put his arms around her, pulling her close gently. He made soothing sounds in her ear until the crying stopped and she raised her head from his shoulder.

"Well, Kass, you give us quite a few day of worry. Are you all right?" Jac asked.

KaSandra smiled through her tear-laden eyelids and accepted the handkerchief that Jac offered. "Oh Jac, it's so good to see someone I know. How did you ever find me and who is Kass?"

"Sure, you can remember his name but not your own. That rich," said Judith as she walked toward the area that Jac and her best friend sat.

KaSandra looked up as Judith approached, and before Judith could reach them, Kass half-screamed as she jumped up and grabbed her friend around the shoulders and said, "Judith." Then looking over Judith's shoulder, she spotted Mike standing next to Tony. Smiling even wider, she released Judith. Half walking, half running, she went over to Mike. Throwing her arms around his neck, she said, "Oh, Mike, now I know how they found me." With her face still shining bright with happiness, she looked at Tony with a question on her face.

Tony stepped forward, saying, "KaSandra, you do not know me. I am Tony Castillo, Jac's uncle."

"So, I finely get to meet you even though this is not the most ideal situation. Jac has mentioned you many times and always stated that he should have you down to the hotel," said Kass.

"Well, I guess you people know each other all right. I will let you get ready to leave," said Dr. Calendar as he walked toward KaSandra and took her hand. Looking directly into her eyes with a smile for the first time, he said, "Miss KaSandra, if you feel comfortable with this situation, why don't you get on with your life. As I said before, your loss of memory is probably not permanent and all should return with time. Just take it easy for about a month, okay?"

"Yes, Dr. Calendar, I understand, and thank you for all your help," returned the very excited KaSandra.

After the doctor left the room, KaSandra turned to the four people still standing or sitting on the other side of the room. With a smile, she said, "KaSandra, KaSandra," as if she had heard it for the first time. "KaSandra Martin, that's my name," she said then laughed. "Mr. Castillo, I believe you are right," the doctor said with a slight German accent.

CHAPTER 11

Leaving the clinic was a great relief to Kass; Jac suggested taking Dr. Calendar's advice of taking some rest in New York with her family. She had not had a vacation for more than a year after leaving her job in Miami. Seeing her parents and friends would probably do her some good, and the hotel will survive.

After a month with family and friends, Kass had been too long away from her friends and her job in Key West. So KaSandra finally said good-bye to her relatives, friends, and the cold weather, and with a queasy stomach—probably the rich food—she caught the next flight to Florida.

As KaSandra rested her head against the headrest with a mystery in her lap, she noticed the seat belt sign turn off. She smiled as she thought of the last five weeks she spent home in Queens. She and her friends ran all over the city, visiting the theaters and nightspots in the evening. The days were for coffeehouses and the endless relatives needing all the gossip of Key West. Finally having enough of the constant bad weather and the endless dry cookies and cake, she was glad to be returning to the Keys and her life. *How had I live all those years, putting up with the relations?*

When she had decided to return to the Keys, she called the hotel to advise them of her return. Jac had said he would meet her flight in Miami and drive her down to the hotel. It had been so good to hear his voice, and as the hours ticked by and the flight got shorter, the excitement mounted inside for she had missed her friends, especially Jac. To keep her mind calm, KaSandra went over all the things she remembered had happen to her before she went away. She remembered leaving the hotel and jumping on the bus to the beach. Then upon arriving, she took off her dress as she walked to her favorite area on the beach, settled down to think, and watched the slow waves as they hit the shore and the rocks not too far away. Her memory of eating her packed sandwich and having ice tea, then strolling along the beach over to the big boulder had come back to her. That had been her usual hike when she visited that area of the beach. She remembered sitting atop the boulder for quite sometime, then turning around and walking back toward her towel and basket. Just then, the plane's landing gear went down, and she felt very queasy again, almost to the point of losing her lunch. As KaSandra walked from the plane ramp and into the arms of the waiting Jac, she forgot all about the sick stomach. She now felt a new pain in her heart.

There in Jac's arms, she thought to herself, *Why can't he see how I feel whenever I'm near him? I only wish I could let him know my true feelings.* Only when she came out of her dream thoughts and looked into Jac's eyes did she notice that he was looking at her in a very different way than he ever had before.

"What were you just thinking about, Kass? The expression on your face was so sweet," asked Jac.

Smiling, KaSandra lied and said, "Oh, how handsome and cool you look in that summer suit. Is it new? It was still very cold and rainy in New York, and it's sure good to be out of that weather and into this warm and sunny weather here."

Again, Jac's instinct told him that she was avoiding his question, but he let it go for to pursue this conversation might cause embarrassment on both sides. He bent and picked up her suitcase where she had dropped it. As he straightened up, he smiled the kind of smile that let most people know that he was not accepting their statement entirely but letting it go for the time being. "It's good to have you back, Kass. You were sorely missed by everyone, and the hotel is in a disastrous condition. Is this the only suitcase that you have?"

"Yes, while I was home packing to come back, I took a real good look at my old clothes and decided to buy all new ones once I got back here. So I guess you're going to have to give me a raise." Jac laughed heartily and put his arm around her shoulder with the intentions of directing her through the crowd of people leaving the airport. After he had held her shoulder for a few minutes, his thoughts started to wander for he liked the way she fit right into his arm as they walked along. KaSandra's thoughts went back to the look that Jac had given her after she lied to him and again felt a rush of warmth for she realized that he didn't fully believe her. If he brings it up again, she was going to tell him the truth.

As the car started over the causeway and into the Keys, KaSandra noticed the weather of Florida like she has never noticed it before. The warmth surrounded her, and all the worries of the past seemed to disappear. She began to feel that she was finally home for the first time in a long time. Jac noticed the smile on her face as she looked at everything that went by and asked her, "Are you glad to be back?" As she smiled back at him, tears filled her eyes, and she whispered, "You will never know how much, Jac. You will never know how much." Handing her his handkerchief and then taking her into his free arm, he whispered back, "Yes, I think I know already."

At the same time, Mike O'Hara was sitting with two new clients in his small, cramped office not far from the hotel, which was the destination for KaSandra and Jac. He was invited to a small get-together at the hotel for the return of KaSandra but now knew he was going to be late. *A perspective job is far more important than putting another ring around my center*, he thought.

CHAPTER 12

The couple that sat across the table from Mike, from the looks of their appearances, was in their early forties and at the peak of their careers. The woman, Alice, wore a very expensive white linen suit, probably a Vanderbilt or Christian Dior, Mike guessed. The blouse she wore was too bright for his taste, but the pattern of linen and silk showed its expensive weave. On her ring finger was a ten-karat diamond, at least, and maybe two karats each in her pierced ears. The man who gave his name as David W. White wore a Calvin Klein or an Armani linen suit. His linen shirt and tie were the top of the line—nothing off the rack for this couple.

They had come to see him about their three-year-old son who was conceived under special reproductive methods. A month ago, he had developed severe appendicitis and had his appendix removed. During the procedure, the Whites found out that the child's blood type did not match either of theirs for he was an AB negative. They were hiring Mike to investigate a local doctor who had done the fertilization procedure on Mrs. White. They loved their son but were very concerned about this situation. They had given Mike a check for $5000 in advance and said they'd be in touch in a month or so for they were off to Morocco for a vacation, just the three of them.

Mike had started an investigation into Dr. Calendar's past just to get a feel about who he is. Since he had come to the Keys, the doc had kept a pretty low profile and made a very lucrative business for himself from all reports. The clinic sat on more than fifty acres of undisturbed grassland and beach. The building itself was made of materials that set right with nature itself and looked quite natural sitting there. It was all on one level with a lot of glass windows and patios, which the patients could use as they recovered from the procedure. From the outside, Mike thought that half the clinic was used for the clinic and half for the personal use of the doctor. Behind the clinic, Mike observed there was a swimming pool, tennis area, and a four-car garage, and he didn't think was for the patients. The back also looked down on the beach and other areas of the Keys. *Yes, indeed the doc was doing quite well for himself*, Mike thought as he sat in his car above the clinic, watching what was going on through field glasses.

Settling back into routine was not as easy as KaSandra thought it would be for she found that the lack of energy she had in New York was the same here. In Queens, she contributed it to the cold weather, but now, she had been back in Key West for almost a month, yet the fatigue and bad stomach had still not gotten better but rather seemed to get worse. What's worse, she believed, is that she had gained weight over the last month.

Sitting with Jac one evening late in the week, she asked him if he had noticed the extra weight she seems to be caring around.

"No, not weight exactly, but I've noticed that you don't seem to concentrate, and you seem on edge since you've gotten back. Is there something I can help you with? Are you still having those nightmares that you had after you returned from the clinic?"

"No, the dreams seem to have disappeared even though I still can't remember all of what happen those three days, except what I told you I did remembered after I got back from New York."

"Yes, I've been thinking about that memory, and there was one thing that struck me as odd about what you said. I hadn't got around to asking you about it."

"What is that, Jac?"

"Well, let me first see if I got it correctly in my mind. You said, I believe, that you remembered turning around and walking back toward you towel and basket after sitting atop the boulder for quite sometime, right?"

"Yes, that right, but nothing after that."

"While you were on the beach, did you see anyone else like a beach comber or a runner getting some exercise?"

"No, Jac, that is a very quiet part of the beach. That is why I like it so much. Why do you ask?"

"Well, I believe that Dr. Calendar mentioned before we entered the room where you were waiting for us that he was running on the beach and found you unconscious by the big boulder. But I could have not heard him correctly."

"How funny. Well, there is one thing I would like to check out if you can spare me tomorrow. I have made an appointment with my doctor for a checkup." After sitting in silence for several minutes, Kass decided to tell Jac her concerns and why she was visiting her doctor.

"Jac, I think we are close enough friends that I can mention my biggest concern to you. You see, I can't remember when I had my last period. At first, I guess it didn't register for I was recovering from my accident and then having a good time with my friends."

"Kass, is that why you are going to the doctor?"

"Yeah, that's one of the reasons, and with this extra weight I have put on, it makes me wonder even more. I hope it is not something serious."

"Now, Kass, don't bring on trouble," said Jac. "I can't see where you've put on any weight, but no need to worry about the time off. Take as much time as you need."

"Thanks, I will only need the afternoon. I think I will turn in now for I am having trouble keeping my eyes open. Jac, you see that is the main reason I am having the physical. I used to be able to stay up all night and never feel tired. Now, here, it is only eleven, and I am just exhausted." She sighed and said, "Good night, Jac" as she got out of her chair and headed for the stairs that led to the first floor.

"Kass," Jac said as he sipped the last of his drink and looked up at her standing on the steps, "let me know what the doctor said after you get back tomorrow, please." Kass nodded her head and went upstairs.

CHAPTER 13

KaSandra finally realized that she was still sitting in her car. Looking at her watch, see found that she had been there two hours. Her appointment with Dr. K. Sharon had been at one o'clock, and now it was four. She still could not believe what the doctor had said to her. It was not possible. *How did this happen to me? I have always been so careful with my relationships, making sure to have protection so nothing like this could happen without my consent. No, the doctor must be wrong, but the tests are so easy and fast now and errorproof that she must be right, and I'm two months pregnant. No! No! It cannot be for I have not had sex in two years. So who was the male that did this to me? How am I going to tell anyone, let alone Jac? Pregnant. I'm pregnant and going to have a baby and have not a clue who the father is.* KaSandra finally got enough energy to get out of the car and walk into the hotel. As she walked, she thought, *I have to find a chair before my wobbly legs gave out, then talk to Jac and try to get an explanation to all this craziness.* The receptionist's voice came out of the fog, saying something about Jac and the bar. She waved her hand in acknowledgment and walked toward the bar.

As she neared the bar, she saw Mike O'Hara sitting with Jac, so she started to turn around to go back to her office. Jac seeing her and raising his voice, said, "KaSandra, come on over here and listen to this story that Mike is telling us about our resident Dr. Calendar."

KaSandra thought, *If I do not go over there and act natural, they will start asking questions, and I do not want a lot of people knowing about my upcoming surprise.* Turning, she walked over to the table, addressing both of her friends, and sat down. Mike took one look at KaSandra and said, "Boy, are you all right? You look like you been fighting and lost."

"Oh, thanks for the compliment, Mike! I am fine, just a little tired and haven't gotten used to the climate here after being in Queens for a month. Mike, please continue with your story about Dr. Calendar that you've been discussing with Jac. I'm very interested in hearing it too."

"Yeah, well first, I should tell you about this couple that got me to investigate him in the first place. It seems that about three years ago, they started seeing the good doctor for help in conceiving a child for they had fertility problems. He is one of the best in the world according to them, and they wanted a child. The Whites finally got their wish and had a son after trying several times with other procedures and spending a lot of money. Everything went along just fine until the boy got appendicitis and received an appendectomy. During the recovery, it came to the couples' notice that their son's blood type didn't match either of theirs. This couple is very proper, and everything has to be just right. They checked with the doctors that have taken care of the families for years and found that the blood type of their son is so different that he would not have been conceived by them. Naturally, they wanted to know what happened and consequently hired me.

"In my investigation so far, I have found that the doctor has had several suits brought against him for misrepresentation. It seems that Dr. Calendar has allegedly been switching the sperm of male clients for his. It never came to trial for the people involved love their children, and after some discussion with the doctor's lawyers, the suits are dropped. Now, it's going to take a little more discussion with my couple for money means nothing to them. Even though they have told me that they love their son and have no intention of losing him, they are really serious about finding out the truth. Well, as serious as they can be for the three of them are out of the country, and I haven't heard a word from them."

"Mike, what proof do you have that Dr. Calendar has been replacing his client's sperms?" asked KaSandra.

"KaSandra, right now, I have nothing that will hold up in court. Most of the people that I've talked to would not talk to me unless it was off the record. I really need a person to come forward and want to take him to trial. Now the clients whom I'm working for, and I have eight of them right now, are hopping mad about the circumstances. I found out that some have already been in contact with the doc's lawyer and received payment or hush money. They might take it further but who knows for they have their reputation to watch out for and that of their precious children."

"Mike, have your clients, the Whites, put a name on what exactly they think the doctor did?" asked Jac.

"Well, that's what I'm trying to find out, but it's not easy for he's covered himself pretty damn well. They think that he either replaced their deposit with someone else's or maybe used his own, so he could be the biological father of their son, not Mr. White.

"I'm on to something right now that I hope will solve this whole problem. If I'm right Dr. Frederick Calendar not only used his own sperm but probably had intercourse with some of his female clients while they were under the anesthesia.

"I've talked with a nurse that quit his service after she got wind of several unethical practices. She couldn't go along with the doctor's practices of having the nurses leave the room just when he was going to implant the eggs and sperm into his female patients. When she questioned the doctor on why he did it for it was against the law to do that, he retorted that it was his clinic and that's the way he wanted it."

"Is this nurse going to give you a statement?" asked Jac.

"Yes, she is willing, but without an actual witness in the room when he was supposed to make the exchange or supply his own form of reproduction, it's just hearsay information and not permissible in court."

"Mike, why is he allegedly doing such things?" Just as KaSandra asked her next question, she shivered for the answer was quite clear before hearing it out loud.

"According to the classmates of his at the Harvard Medical School, that's quite easy to answer. It seems that Dr. Frederick Calendar was always under the opinion that he is a genius, so his genes should continue even if he doesn't want children of his own. They use to laugh at him and ask him how he was going to do this. They never took what he said as gospel until all those law suits were brought against him. They didn't say anything because all the people suing him suddenly dropped their claims. The only way I can think of getting a conviction is to catch him in the act, or getting his blood type to match with the children's would work."

"Aren't there records somewhere with his blood type written down?" As KaSandra was talking, her voice was showing more and more stress, which did not go unnoticed by the two people listening. "Like the military or some hospital records that could prove he's the father of these children." KaSandra found that tears were streaming down her face before she realized what was happening and could stop herself. Jac was instantly kneeling beside her and asking with a lot of concern in his voice, "Kass, what is the matter? Can we help? Is it the results of your doctor's appointment?"

All KaSandra could do was shake her head for she was not sure she wanted to speak about her news in front of Mike. In her heart, she knew that it was the only solution to how she got pregnant. The next second, she was handed a glass of whiskey by

Mike and asked, "KaSandra, would you rather I left so you can talk to Jac in private?"

"No, Mike, please stay. I think what I have to say will need the two of you to solve. Sit down, Mike, and you too Jac for this is going to take awhile," said the now-under-control KaSandra as she set the glass on the table.

"Mike, you didn't know until Jac asked me about my doctor's appointment today. I was with my gynecologist, Dr. K. Sharon, for I thought I had something wrong with my menstrual cycle. It is far worse than I thought. I am going to join your list of clients against Dr. Fredrick Calendar. You see, I'm going to have a baby, and he has to be the father. It's the only possibility that I can come up with. I've been sitting in my car since my doctor's appointment, trying to figure out how this could have happened. I have been leading a celibate life for the last two years, so how did I get pregnant? Then you started telling me about your case against Dr. Calendar. It all made sense. I still can't remember what happened to me or how I got to the clinic. I was there three days, and that give that bastard plenty of time to do his worse before you found me." There was a long silence as the three people sat and stared into space, thinking their own thoughts. Mike finally broke the silence by saying, "Well, what are you going to do about your situation?"

"Situation is right," said Jac, pounding his fist down on the table top. "When I get that guy in my hands, I going to make sure he won't have a chance to have any more kids." Then he noticed the two faces that were staring at him in wonderment from the other side of the table, and he started to cry. "I am so angry at what he did to you that I can't wait to see him in jail for good," Jac said through his tears. In an instance, both Mike and Kass had their arms around Jac, and Kass said, "That is just what you and Mike are going to do, Jac, with all of our help, and to answer you question Mike, are you asking if I am going to have this baby or not? Well, my answer is yes. I'm in my mid-thirties, and my possibility of having children is getting smaller. This baby is a gift in that respect, but I don't want that Calendar to get away with what he did to me."

"KaSandra, you have my support if that is your decision. I can only think of one other person who'd be a better mother than you, and that's my own mother. I promise you that I will do everything in my power to get to the truth and put Dr. Calendar behind bars," said Mike.

CHAPTER 14

"It's odd, KaSandra," said Mike, "but I hope you tell your child when he/she are old enough what its father did to you just as another mother did not tell Calendar."

"Ah, what do you mean?" asked Kass.

"There is a story that I dug up about the doctor that I'd like to tell you even though it won't help what he's done to you. It seems that his mother, who lives in Germany, never was married to his father. From what I've found out, he may not even know which male friend of his mother was his father. Her maiden name was Gretchen Mueller, and she supposedly was a real beauty but born on the wrong side of society and dirt poor. The only thing that saved her from utter starvation was her brains and good looks. The story goes from old neighbors that she left home really early, about fourteen, heading for Bonn and a job as a model and ended up selling herself to stay alive. I learned from an old roommate that she met this baron and supposedly got married to him. Anyway, she found her way to England, with her baron, and got connected to the best-known model agency before she was sixteen. The baron, it seems, found someone more to his liking, or not as ambitious, and left Gretchen to her own devising with a tidy sum at her disposal. Remember, this as no wallflower, but she was like many youngsters who don't know how to control their lives after the money starts rolling in from the modeling. She did almost everything to excess: food, drugs, sex, and then there was William, the camera man who got her in the family way and left.

The baron was long gone for he had found a wealthy woman in London and arrangements were made to annul his relationship with Gretchen, providing her with an ample settlement according to another storyteller and quickly married his new companion.

"This left Gretchen out of liquid money, and soon her pregnancy would show and end her modeling career. She knew Charles Calendar, who was part of her clubbing crowd and came from a very good family socially and was very wealthy. Charles worked in freelancing but what exactly no one wants to talk about. Gretchen convinced him that the baby was his, and he married her, and they both immigrated to the United States. He was persuaded that the marriage and move would preserve his family's good name, and Gretchen could get away from the kind of life she had gotten caught up into.

"Once in the United States, Charles, who was not accustomed to working, did not do so well, and the settlement that his family provided was running out. So he found his solace in the areas he was acquainted with and started his old life's activities of easy money in his new city. Gretchen had since delivered Frederick and found work as a model with one of the top agency in New York and soon moved up to being a top model. Her success did not help the disposition of Charles, and Frederick seemed to be Charles's only comfort. Frederick bloomed with the affection shown to him by his father and soon became his father's son. Gretchen found herself out of the lives of both her husband and son, but with her career in full gear and her drifting away from the family, she didn't seem to mind that she didn't matter to the men in her life.

"With his son to raise and care for, Charles soon found his way of life out of control. He wanted to be a good father, and he turned his interests to becoming a minister of God. Charles always had a magnetic personality and did quite well in getting followers to join his ministry. He stopped drinking and divorced Gretchen on the ground of abandonment. He won custody of

Frederick, but with his long record of alcoholism, Gretchen received generous visitation rights and lavished attention and gifts on her son.

"Then Charles married a woman by the name of Magdaleana Olson. She came from a family of very orthodox believers and was also the child of a minister. Her father believed that his daughters should and would not be allowed in the presence of a male outside their family members. Any question to do with sex was a forbidden topic, and anyone, especially men, who were sexually active, such as Charles Calendar, were supposedly evil. Minister Olson was caught up in Charles's magnetism and ability to draw the correct people into the ministry. He also liked the idea that his new fellow minister was quite an eligible male with a small son to raise, so he immediately introduced him to his oldest daughter, Magdaleana.

"Magdaleana, because of her upbringing, had never refused her father's wishes for he knew what was best for his daughters. At her father's request, she married Minister Charles Calendar, though she neither know nor loved him.

"Within a week of marriage, she felt betrayed by her father. Her new spouse was not the man he pretended to be. She found out to her horror that she was married to a man who enjoyed sex and wanted it quite frequently with frills. A strong believer of the fact that the man was the head of the household and to be obeyed in all things only strengthened her betrayal. Her strong religious beliefs forbade her the strength to act differently, and so she followed her upbringing to the letter, even if not necessarily done in good faithful acts. She had learned that Frederick was conceived without the benefit of marriage and blamed him, not her husband, for the sin. Shortly after her marriage to Charles, she found out that she would never be able to carry a child to birth. After having a miscarriage in her first month, the doctor said she was just too small, and with this news, Magdaleana became more embittered against Frederick. Charles was pleased with the news that his second wife was unproductive for it freed him to guide his woman parishioners into areas for his discreet pleasure. He also started directing his only child into the areas that he thought suitable for the son of a minister. This was in the ways of money, education, and influence to get what you wanted. This would mark Frederick for the rest of his life for his father insisted on his strict authority while his actions showed another way to life. Frederick also got the wrong view of what marriage and the relationship with women was all about. His stepmother's bitterness toward him and the overindulgence of his mother warped his thoughts on women. As he reached puberty, his natural sexual urges further complicated his warped sexual feelings, and because of the constant intercession of his free-spirited mother on one side and his stringent stepmother on the other, he found himself constantly searching for sexual release.

"What drew the teenager was the darker side of his father's life, and with the monetary help from his mother his high school years were carefree. Surprisingly, it was his stepmother's uneven hatred for herself and him that spurred him into the medical profession. Magdaleana's malice for her stepson and the shame she felt for not being able to carry a baby to full term spurred his genius mind and appetite to the way of helping women get pregnant artificially. Using his mother's money from the modeling agency she now owned. Frederick entered Harvard Medical School at the age of twenty and proceeded to be the top of his class. Six years later, he finished at Harvard School of Medicine, including an internship at New York Presbyterian Hospital, and soon became one of the world's highest-paid physicians in the area of infertility and artificial insemination. He started caring for couples who are unable to conceive, while his perverted mind allegedly drove him to produce offspring in his own image, taking his pleasure's it seemed, with his unsuspecting clients. He either placed his sperm in the petri dish to inject or had sex with the clients while under the anesthetic."

Mike stared off into space as he finished the last sentence of his story about Dr. Frederick Calendar. All who were sitting around the small table in the salon of the bar were silent. Judith, who had joined the group just as Mike was relating his story, had missed KaSandra's disclosure to Mike and asked, "Why, Mike, are you talking about the Dr. Calendar? What is up?"

Everyone looked at Judith, and KaSandra was the first to find her voice. "Well, Judith, it seems that our illustrious Dr. Calendar has been forming babies in his own image ever since he started his practice as a doctor."

"Now, KaSandra, that's not a proven fact," said Mike.

"Oh, yes, it is, and I'm the proof. How else would I be pregnant?"

"What!" was all Judith could say after she heard the news. Now, it was Judith's turn to regain her voice, and she said, "I had a feeling when he shook my hand at the clinic that there was something evil about that man."

"The question is now what are we going to do about it?" said Jac.

"That is simple," said Judith. "We will just catch him in the act. I also noticed the way he looked at me as he held my hand in his. I can go out there and ask for an examination on the presumption that I would like to conceive without the benefit of a partner and after trying several times without success with my ex-lover, have decided that I do not need a man to have a baby of my own.

"Is there not a way for us to get a couple of doctors to say that I have already tried to get pregnant under their care and it just does not seem to work? Women are having and raising babies all the time now without a man's help, so I have decided to get artificially inseminated if I am a candidate. I just supposedly need a little more help," said Judith. "Jac, you must know some doctors who owes you a favor or maybe your godfather, that wonderful-looking Tony Castillo."

Everyone was so shocked that Judith would even think of such a plan, let alone be the subject involved. From the surprise, it took several minutes for anyone to speak after Judith was silent.

Mike finally said, "It just might work. We'd have to work out all the details down to the smallest fact so nothing could go wrong, but it just might work."

"Are are you two crazy? Judith, absolutely not," said Jac. "It's far too dangerous, and you might end up in the same situation that KaSandra's in."

"Jac, I am going through with it. I do not think it will ever get that far, but to be even more safe, can we get his routine from one of his nurses or staff?"

"Mike, would that nurse you told us about be able to give us that information?" asked KaSandra

"Well, Ms. ah, let me see here…" Mike reached into his pocket and pulled out his notepad. "Ms. Central. Yes, Wendy Central, RN, told me over the phone that she would give me a statement. I could get a hold of her and ask for the routine and procedure used by her ex-employer. I believe she told me that he let her go without even severance pay or the two-week notice she was entitled to. It's worth a try for she didn't sound too happy about the situation the last time we talked."

"Judith, why do you want to do this for me?" asked KaSandra.

"It is not just you, Kass. This is the second time a doctor has taken advantage of a friend of mine and got away with it. Back in my old neighborhood, my best friend fell for her doctor in a big way, and he got her pregnant at the age of fourteen and then left her high and dry. Now, we have this doctor disrupting lives, and he will not get away with it. I was too young to help the other person, but all the right ingredients are available for a good sting, and it is about time someone puts a bad doctor out of business."

"What can I do?" asked KaSandra.

"You could pay a visit with Mike to see this nurse, Ms. Wendy Central, and tell her the situation so we can increase our chances of getting her help," said Jac.

"Oh, are you with us now, boss?" asked KaSandra and Judith in unison.

"I don't have anything to do right now, and I don't want you three to have all the fun. We need those medical records for Judith, and I believe I know just the right person to help us out. Mike, you will have to get to your clients and any of the other couples that the doctor helped and most likely paid off when they got suspicious of wrong doing, and see if they are really willing to help us. Maybe Ms. Central will be able to help us there also, with the dates on when the clients got inseminated."

"If they can all get together with my godfather and tell him their stories, I am sure he knows someone of good influence that can help us out at the right time. We are also going to have to get Judith next to the doctor and get him interested in doing something about her too."

Jac took a look at his watch and said, "Hey it's getting late in the evening. How about all of us getting something to eat and discussing this further?"

"That sounds like a good idea. I starved all of a sudden, and I'm eating for two now," said KaSandra.

They all laughed as they got up to go into the dining room. Jac suggested that Kass not tell anyone else that she was going to have a baby for if the wrong person heard, they might spoil the trap on Dr. Calendar.

Jac, sitting with his friends, just finishing a delicious meal created by the extraordinary hands of Joe Cartage, his Paris-taught chef and bodyguard for the hotel staff, even though it was without their knowledge. Before Joe took up cooking for a career with one of the finest houses in France, where he became one of their top chefs, he had been a top contender for the Golden Buckle. He gave it up after he was hit square in the jaw, which left him unconscious for two hours, and the doctor said another hit like that would end not only his career but his life. Leaving Paris for the States after learning all he could from the finest of the finest in the culinary field, he was picked up for vagrancy and was going to be deported when Jac stepped in and hired him for his hotel.

These pleasant moments were about to be shattered because a block away from the spot where Jac sat was a man all dressed in black, laying eight sticks of dynamite to destroy one more item that Jac owned. That act of destruction brought Jac back to the reality that his past will always be with him no matter how hard he try to bury it.

At exactly eight p.m., a bomb brought the brick storage building and boat dock on the waterfront of the hotel to their eradication. The bomber had been hired by Jac's old nemesis to get Jac's attention and let him know that he, Kaper, was back and that the game was to start again.

CHAPTER 15

Kaper Kalabrese was Jac's challenger. They were once best friends in the early days, back in Syracuse, New York, where they both went to Theodore Roosevelt High School. Kaper came from a very affluent family, the only child of a debutante mother and a father who owned several banks in New York. Even though Kaper got whatever he ask for he was expected to come in number one in everything he tried.

Upon entering his freshman year of high school, along with Jac and many more boys he knew from middle school, Kaper was always making himself out to be number one in everything he tried for it was expected of him. Trying out for the football team was his first goal, but there was Jac, and he got a position too. Jac went on to become the team's captain in his junior and senior years in football, and Kaper had to settle for the baseball team and captain only in his senior year. This did not please his father. Then when Jac and Kaper tried out for the lead in the junior class play of Hamlet, Jac got the part of Hamlet. It wasn't that Jac was better than Kaper for they were both good students, but Jac was a friend to all the guys, while Kaper had a tough time seeing all of them as equals. After the Hamlet lead went to Jac, Kaper's father took his new Porsche away from him for six months. Kaper blamed Jac, and if Kaper did happen to outdo Jac and pass him up for some honor, it seemed to Kaper that Jac got the lion's share of the attention.

In their senior year, Kaper and Jac were both nominated for king of the prom. This time, Kaper won the crown, but the queen only had eyes for Jac all night long. This is when Kaper's grudge against Jac took on a different meaning. They had always had their differences, but that night, Kaper had plans for his queen, and she ended up leaving with Jac.

This is not to say that Jac did not have his revenge. The first small escalation of their animosity occurred after Kaper's father took the Porsche away. Jac found all his tires deflated and knew it had been Kaper. He also knew that the only transportation that Kaper had was his motorbike, and the bike ended up with sugar in its gas tank. Then there was the Saran Wrap all over Jac's car after Kaper was turned down for a date when Jac had asked the girl first. Jac took whipping cream and gave the sheen of the Porsche a second skin, and the pranks of teenage years cost muscle and hard work to put things back to order.

It was the animosity of manhood that started escalating the dollars into hundreds of thousands. After Jac's hotel was burnt to the ground, he retaliated by burning down Kaper's five hundred thousand-dollar Maine cabin that was taken next on the score card. The only addition to this escapade was that Kaper was brought up on tax evasion, which the FBI found during their investigation on his cabin's burning. Kaper got five years in a country club prison for tax evasion. He was out in three years. The cabin was stated as faulty fireplace flue that caught fire from the old timber.

Now that Kaper was out of prison, he had renewed their grudge validation for he hired someone to blow up Jac's boathouse just to let Jac know that he was back and ready to continue the rancor match.

Jac knew who was responsible as he walked through the destruction. He now had to make a decision to either escalate the feud or find some solution that would end it for good. As he turned to walk back to the hotel and come up with a plan, he saw something wedged between a brick and a fallen wood. He bent to retrieve it and found a wallet. Opening the flap, Jac realized that the contents had not been damaged by the fire. The owner's name on the driver's license was a Thomas Lesueur.

As Jac reached his office, he met Mike, who was just about to walk in, and said, "You are just the person I was looking for, Mike. I would like you to check with that friend of yours in the police department and see if you can find anything on a Thomas Lesueur."

"Thomas Lesueur," Mike whistled under his breath. "What do you want with that loser?"

"I don't, but I found his wallet in the rubble of my burnt-out boathouse and need to find him before he leaves town."

"You mean he was the one? What does he have against you?"

"No, he was just the hired firebug. The person who did that," Jac pointed out the window at the wharf, "was a schoolmate of mine. He has held a grudge against me since we were in high school together. We used to go back and forth with little pranks, but the situation got out of hand. He ended up in prison for tax evasion, and now he is out. I don't really want to send him back to prison, but I will if it comes down to me losing any more property."

"What do you mean 'any more property'?" asked Mike.

"Well, the police think that my hotel burning down two years ago was just an accident with faulty wiring that had not been replaced. It wasn't an accident. It was Kaper."

"I wondered why you never put in for your insurance."

"Well, I really couldn't because then the police or FBI would find out about our little games of one-upmanship, and Kaper would not be the only one going to prison. Just like that mess, again pointing to the destruction, the police will not find out about this stunt. Right?" said Jac.

"Say, I'm in private investigation now, not on the police force," said Mike.

Jac, thinking out loud, said, "Yes, the two of us are going to find Mr. Lesueur before Kaper or someone else does. First, scare the life out of him so badly that he comes clean and identifies Kaper as the instigator even though we have him dead to rights with his driver's license here." Jac started going through the contents in the wallet compartment. "Look, here is a receipt for a motel in Long Pine Keys."

"It's a place to start," said Mike.

"Mr. Kalabrese please. Thomas Lesueur. Yes, I can hold."

"Mr. Lesueur, did our little project go boom, boom?"

"It's all taken cared of, and the view from the hotel is no longer obstructed. Was my ten grand put in the Vegas bank under the name of Thomas Brown like I asked?"

"It was all taken cared of," said Kaper. "What are you going to do now?"

"Oh, I thought I'd go over to the gulf and do some deep sea fishing maybe near St. Petersburg or Clearwater."

"Sounds like a relaxing idea, good fishing."

Thomas walked out of the motel after paying his bill and headed for his rental car. Popping the truck, he placed his suitcase and fishing equipment in. Thomas though he could rent the equipment he didn't have to catch the bigger fish. Looking up, he noticed a man standing next to the driver's side door. The hairs on the back of his head stood right up, and he knew from experience that this meant trouble. This man was either a cop or something worse. He smiled and said just as calmly as he could even though he wasn't feeling too calm, "Can I help you mister?"

Mike just smiled back and said, "Yes, if you are Thomas Lesueur."

"Lesueur, no, sorry. My name is Thomas Brown. What do you want with this Mr. Lesueur just in case I run into him?"

"Oh, not much, I just wanted to return his wallet to him. You see, it was found on the beach down at a hotel on the Keys, and inside was a receipt for this motel. I guess I must have missed him even though the clerk at the front desk said he just checked out."

"Let's say that I might know of this Thomas Lesueur, what would you be wanting with him other than to give him back his wallet?"

"Oh, there is a friend of mine back at that hotel who would like a little information about an explosion done to his property. He thinks that maybe this Thomas Lesueur would know something about it or maybe he'd know who ordered the incident to happen." Thomas got quite frightened about the information that Mike had just told him and started looking around to see if he could get away.

Mike, thinking that this firebug might take flight, continued talking, "You see, this friend of mine would be willing to pay for this information without implicating this Mr. Lesueur."

This caught Thomas's attention, and he said, "What kind of payments are we taking about, and why would he be willing to pay for it?"

"Well, it seems that the owner of the hotel is not too concerned with the building being destroyed as much as he is in implicating the person who hired the demolition. Since I've missed this man, I guess I'll just look further." Mike turned to walk away, and Thomas step in his path. "If I was this Lesueur person, what kind of money are we talking about? You see, it has to be worth my while to turn on the person who employed me to do the job."

"Are you saying that you are this Thomas Lesueur and for money now would be willing to return to the Keys and talk with my friend who owned the structures that were destroyed?"

"Wait, wait. How much dough we are talking here? After all, I was given ten big ones to blow the buildings. I should get that much for squealing on the person who hired me and the danger I'm putting myself into."

"Yes," said Mike, "I think the owner would be willing to cover that sum. But you would have to come with me right now, and let us tape your whole story from start to finish and name names. What to you say to that?"

"Okay, you've got yourself a deal. Do we drive my car or yours?"

"We'll take my car and drive all night, and then you can get back to wherever you were heading. Go and call the car agency to pick up their car in the office, and I'll place your belongings in my trunk," and Mike stressed this point, "See you outside the motel's front in a couple of minutes, okay?"

"Sure, sure, I'll see you out front. Oh, by the way, what do folks call you anyway?"

"O'Hara. You can call me O'Hara."

CHAPTER 16

Mike and Thomas Lesueur walked across the hotel's lobby and into Jac's office just as he was replacing the phone receiver into its cradle. Jac had just been talking to his godfather, Anthony Castello, about the progress he was having with the doctor in New York who owed him some favors. The doctor was willing to sign an affidavit that stated that a Ms. Judith Polymer was diagnosed with a physical ailment called endometriosis and that this prevented her from conceiving the natural way. Tony had promised the doctor that the letter would never get into the wrong hands and that after it was no longer needed, it would be destroyed. Jac had called Tony the week before to discuss the KaSandra's situation. He was asking for Tony's help on starting a sting that included Judith's plan. This meant that Tony would be calling in some of his IOUs in getting some medical help. Jac related to his uncle the list of victims that Mike had compiled. Jac stated that Mike had asked all these people to contact Tony if they were willing to get involved in stopping others from getting hurt. Mike confirmed that he thought that most of them had been terribly hurt and got no justice after being intimidated into silence or paid.

Tony told Jac that he had already received calls from the nine couples on Mike's list and arranged with them to come to his home for a meeting. He was going to let them get together and discuss how they were going to stop Dr. Calendar from hurting any more people. Tony thought that Mike, KaSandra, Judith, and

Jac—if he could find the time in his busy day—should come over in the morning so they can discuss the sting with his guests.

Jac looked up from his chair behind the mahogany desk in his office and asked Mike while completely ignoring Thomas, "Is this our Mr. Lesueur, and is he willing to help us?"

"Hey, you know, I'm not someone you talk around or ignore," said Thomas. "I'm here to do you a favor and could get killed for it."

Jac smiled at Thomas. "Who is doing whom a favor?" Jac got up out of the chair and walked across to the window that looked out onto the beach and the now-cleared place that was once his boat dock and storage area.

"Listen, this private dick here said you would be willing to give me ten grand to come back and give taped testimony against the person who hired me," Thomas said.

"Ten. I'm afraid you will have to do more than just give testimony for that kind of money," said Jac. "I do to need your help on another little deal that is right up your alley." Thomas started to back away from the desk toward the door. Mike barred his way and guided him to a chair that was in front of Jac's desk, keeping his hand on Thomas's shoulder.

"You have caused me a great deal of money and time with your actions the other night," Jac said to Thomas while he was still facing the window. Turning slowly and walking back to his brown leather chair, he looked down at Thomas and started to stare at him until he squirmed under the look.

"Okay, what exactly do you want me to do other than the testimony?" Thomas asked.

"Right now, I want you to loosen up but stay around the hotel. I'll book you a room here and tell the front desk that you are my guest. I'll also start a limited bar and food tab of five hundred dollars that will come out of the money you are expecting. There is someone here in the hotel that is going to be your shadow, so don't try to leave or do anything that would make him angry. He could break you like a twig. Do you understand?"

"Sure," said Thomas. "Could I put a start on that tab right now at the bar? I'm kinda thirsty."

"Certainly, you're my visitor," said Jac.

The company that Anthony Castello was expecting arrived late on that warm April evening. The first to arrive by private jet were David and Alice White, followed by the Egans, Mary and Robert, who had been vacationing in Miami when Tony's service caught up to them. They drove down to Tony's estate in their Mercedes. Armon Kleins and Patrick Dugans had called and would be arriving late in the Keys, most likely around 11:00 p.m. They would find a place to stay overnight and arrive early the next morning. Peter Brown called and said that Linda's mother had died but that they wanted to be included in any arrangements that would put the doctor behind bars. Mrs. Brown was most outspoken about being kept abreast of the situation. Mr. Charles Chart said he and his wife, Doris, would think about it. A definite no, thought Tony. Tony talked to a Mrs. Duncan Fiscal of Elgin, Illinois who, was angered by the suggestion of doing anything against Dr. Calendar for he provided them with the opportunity to conceive a wonderful daughter. Mrs. Fiscal explained that her husband was out of the country, but she was sure he would feel the same way. She also asked Tony not to bother them with the subject again. Tony's service never got a hold of the Clarks, so Tony thought he would try but had no success.

The morning of the meeting, Mike phoned to let Tony know that he, Wendy Central, and KaSandra would be there around 9:30 a.m. for a talk with his guests. Mike asked if he had located everyone on the list, and Tony told him that only two couples had not been contacted, the Farmingtons of Farmington, Missouri, and the Clarks of Seattle, Washington. Mike then told Tony that Jac had hired a man by the name of Lesueur to help on the sting. After Mike had finished telling Tony what had occurred in Long Pine Keys and how he and Jac had convinced Lesueur to play ball with them, Tony asked, "Are you sure you can trust this bum?"

"Oh sure, he really wants the money, and he probably knows that he won't get any more out of Kaper."

"I warned Jac years ago," said Tony, "that this game he was playing with Kaper would someday come down around his head. I hope he realizes this now, and the best situation is to help him bring these games to an end before he lands in prison for something I can't help with."

"Right," said Mike.

"Mike, you are a great friend. See you at the meeting."

After Mike finished his conversation with Tony, he walked back to the kitchen in the hotel to talk with Joe. As he entered the kitchen, Joe was pouring a cup of coffee and raised an empty cup at Mike. Mike replied with, "Sure Joe, I need some coffee. Only wish there was something stronger in it." Without a hesitation, Joe reached under the counter and pulled out a bottle of Johnny Walker Red Label and offered it to Mike, saying, "Will this do?"

"Do? That's treating me like royalty. Are you having any?"

"You bet, I never let a fellow drink alone if I can help it," said Joe with a laugh. "What brings you back here? Can you smell the shrimp out in the hotel?" Joe knew that Mike's second love was that scavenger of the deep, especially when he was hungry. "Nope, just wanted to check on Jac's guest and see if he's behaving himself."

"Behaving, are you kidding? He thinks he's King Tut. Been lounging out on the beach, soaking up the sun, and ordering drinks and food like there's no tomorrow," said Joe. Mike started laughing and almost choked on a fresh bit of shrimp that Joe had just served to him.

"Joe, I sure hope that Jac has thought about what would happen if Kaper gets wind of what he has done in hiring this guy to spill his guts on how he was hired to blow up the boat landing. For Kaper, this could easily just accelerate his revenge on Jac," said Mike.

"I thought that was what Jac was trying to do. End this feud and let this so-called buddy of his know the game is over," said Joe.

Mike nodded with his mouth full of shrimp. "Yes, but he has been so busy with this business of KaSandra's that he hasn't gotten a stenographer in here to take Lesueur's testimony."

"Heck Mike," said Joe, "I think Crystal, our receptionist, is ah, ah, what you called it, and she can type too."

"Well, thanks Joe. I'll mention it to Jac." Mike wiped his mouth and stood up and as he turned to walk out. He stopped, and looking toward his friend, he said, "Thanks, Joe, that sauce on the shrimp was just hot enough. Oh, keep a close eye on King Tut."

CHAPTER 17

Thomas Lesueur sat on the beach under an umbrella for the noon sun was now very hot and he didn't want to ruin his almost-perfect tan. As he sat there, staring out at the waves that made a constant splash against the rocks, his thoughts turned to the trouble he was now in, too deep to get out of since he answered the questions about how he had blown up the boat dock and the connecting buildings. Mr. Scarin had outlined what his new position was going to involve, as the women who sat there, making a constant clickety-clack on that machine that was recording his every word, made him feel his life was not worth a plug nickel. The job that was described to him seemed interesting enough, right up his alley. He always enjoyed a good con more than blowing up some stupid building. "Oh, what the heck. You can't live forever," Thomas said out loud and started looking around again for that big bosomy blond whom he had seen earlier.

He spotted the blond again leaning against the bar. Thomas flexed his arm muscles, and the tattoo *Mom* came to life. Thomas had always considered himself to be a ladies man after all. He thought, *Here, I am lean, muscles galore, great tan, and all the women say I have a tiny ass. Why that's so important to them, I'll never know, but I'm not complaining, not one little bit.* He got up from his lounge chair and walked over to the bar, taking the seat right next to the blond.

The blond Mabel had noticed Thomas before, when she first came down to sunbathe, and had taken a seat at the bar, hoping he would make a move on her before she was forced to start some action of her own.

Watching him like a hawk out of the corner of her eye as he stretched and flexed those tattooed arms, Mabel thought that, that body of his was just what she had been looking for; his height and weight also suited her nicely. *He sure must have love his mother to put that beautiful tattoo on himself*, she pondered. Then she noticed he was getting ready to leave and hoped he was coming to introduce himself and maybe even buy her a drink. Mabel adjusted her bathing suit top and ran her tongue over her front teeth to make sure there was no lipstick on them. When he sat down on the stool next to hers, Mabel's heart beat so fast and loud that she was sure he could hear it. She tried not to give him notice as he hailed the bartender to bring him another drink and then turned to her and asked, "Say pretty, can I buy you a drink?"

Mabel was not sure how he was going to address her but had to laugh when he called her pretty. "That would be very nice. Do you really think I'm pretty?" she said as she looked him full in the face.

"Pretty, hell yes." His eyes fell to her very large breast that would pop out of her suit if she took a big breath. His thoughts wandered as he noticed the bartender pouring the liquor into the empty glasses then placed it in front of them. *Boy would I like to slide my hand right down the side of her suit and around one of those beauties. If we were alone, I'd do just that and pop the other one of them out right into my other waiting hand just to feel their silkiness*, Thomas thought.

Mabel had noticed his quietness and glanced out the corner of her eye to see what he was doing. Noticing that his eyes were on her front, she took a small breath that was just enough to make her breast rise a little, and she heard him catch his breath as he flexed his muscles, making his tattoos jump. It was then that she noticed his other tattoo on the inside of his left arm. It was a big, red heart with the words *hot lover* written across it. "Oh, that's wonderful. May I touch it?" Mabel said as she reached for his arm. Thomas's eyes left her front and traveled down her arm as she reached for his tattoo. He felt her finger as she touched his skin, and he flexed his arm muscle without thinking for his eyes were on the diamond ring that graced her long but fat fingers. "Wow," he said to himself. "That must be at least fourteen carats."

Mabel could not help giggling as she felt his skin ripple under her finger. "That's really neat, and thanks for the drink." She rested her hand on his thigh and looked into his eyes with a smile and said, "Are you staying here at the hotel?"

"Yeah, I have a room on the second floor. How about you?" he said and smiled so big, all his upper teeth showed.

"Oh, no, not me," said Mabel. "I'm staying with a friend here on the Keys, but I like this beach front so much better then hers that I always come down here to sunbathe."

"Oh, if you have some free time now, might there be a possibility the two of us could have dinner together?" said Thomas.

"That's a wonderful idea, but I'm not dressed for the dining room."

"Well, I'm not either, so maybe I could put you into a taxi and see you about seven for a few drinks, dinner, dancing, and then let nature take its course. What do you say?"

Mabel's eyes started to sparkle, and she smiled a great big smile in anticipation. "I have my car here," she said as she slipped off the stool and bent to pick up her beach bag, almost falling out of her suit top. As she straightened up, she noticed Thomas's eyes had strayed to her bosoms again, so she took another breath to make them bounce. "I'll see you at seven," Mabel said with another bright smile. Without waiting for his comment, she turned and walked toward the parking lot. Thomas noticed as he watched her walk away that his palms were wet with sweat, and he was glad that his suit was still a little wet for the front of him sure felt like it.

CHAPTER 18

Jac held the phone to his ear and listened to the ring, counting each one and hoping there would not be an answering machine. Suddenly, there was a pickup and a voice answered, saying, "Kaper Kalabrese here."

"Kaper, Jac Scarin. I'm glad I caught you in town."

"Well, Jac, your voice was the last one I thought I'd hear. What can I do for you?" Kaper voice might have sounded light and full of life, but his face took on a deep, ugly glare.

Jac took a deep breath, which he hoped would not be detected, and said, "Kaper, I thought maybe you and I could get together somewhere at your convenience to talk about stopping this ridiculous feud for we are not boys anymore."

"Oh, Jac, my boy, I'm just getting started. I've waited two long years, just dreaming and planning how I was going to get back at you for sending me to prison. When I'm finished with you, everything you own will be demolished."

"Kaper, think about this a little longer. In the first place, I didn't send you to prison. The feds did for tax evasion. We are now grown adults, and your father is deceased, so you have nothing to prove. I must say that if you keep this game going, you will end up back in prison for a lot longer than two years."

"No, Jac, this time, if I go to prison again, I won't be alone. You will be sharing the next cell. Remember old friend, your hands are also soiled with dynamite and other nasty little things."

"Kaper, let's get together and talk about this."

"I've talked and waited long enough. The next bang is going to be that red car of yours or maybe the hotel again. Still want to talk? I think there's been enough talking, Jac. I'm just going to get even now."

"Kaper, before you hang up, may I say one more thing?"

"Sure, Jac. Sure, what is it? More pleading?" Jac heard an evil laugh on the other end of the phone.

"Thomas Lesueur."

Kaper's laughter ended with a jolt, and all was quiet on the other end of the phone. "Is that supposed to mean something to me?" he said.

"I hope so, Kaper, old friend. I have a signed affidavit from Thomas Lesueur, explaining how you hired him to blow up my dock, storage building, and boats. I also have a signed receipt in your name from the bank in Vegas, authorizing the transfer of ten grand into the account of Thomas Brown, a.k.a. Thomas Lesueur. Need I go any further? Now, will you think about calling off this senseless game before someone really gets hurt?"

"I will think about it." There was a click, and the phone in Jac's hand went dead. Jac sat there for at least three minutes with the phone in his hand before he was aware that he was still holding on to it. His thoughts were back in his youth when he and Kaper were in school together and this whole situation started. *You really can't blame the situation on any one thing or person*, he thought. There was Kaper's father, who was always pushing him to be the best in everything and was always disappointed. Kaper could never seem to make his old man happy and went so far as threatening Kaper with disinheritance when he fell short. *Kaper's father has been dead ten months now, and Kaper is still holding on to this hatred toward me. No, it can't just be that he spent the last two years in prison. It has to be something else. I just haven't figured it out.*

The buzz of the phone's intercom brought Jac back to reality, and realizing the phone was still in his hand, he answered the intercom. "Jac here."

"Hi, Jac, this is KaSandra. Are you too busy for a short conversation?"

Jac opened the door after hanging up the phone and found Kass sitting on the receptionist desk, swinging her legs back and forth just like a little girl. The sight made him laugh out load and in doing so caught Kass's attention, who was still holding the phone to her ear, waiting for his reply.

"Are you laughing at me?" Kass asked with a smile as she removed herself from the tabletop and replaced the phone in its cradle.

"Oh, never." Jac grinned. "How about going to the restaurant and having some coffee while we talk?"

"Sure." Kass slipped her arm through Jac's arm and said with a big smile, "I'll even buy."

As they reached the restaurant, they met Judith, who was just coming up with an arm full of supplies for the bar. "What are you two up to? It looks like no good from the expressions on your faces."

Kass smiled at Judith and replied, "Oh, not too much." Realizing that she had been flirting with Jac and embarrassed that she had gotten caught in the act, she said, "I thought that the three of us could get together for a meeting. We need to go over what we are going to discuss tonight at Anthony's meeting with the aggrieved couples."

"Say, that is a good idea. I am getting excited about my part in this sting. Grab a table, and I will get coffee for all. Oh, here comes Mike," said Judith.

"Judith, are you sure you want to go through with your end of this operation?" asked Jac. "We still have time to get someone else."

"Someone else? Not on your life! All I have to do is go up there and pretend that I want to get pregnant by artificial means. You know that Tony has received those phony medical records in my name. That should be enough proof that I am serious about having a child without sex in my life."

"Yes, that's true, but I saw the way the doc looked at you when we were up there to bring Kass back," said Jac. "From the reports that Mike has provided about this guy, he has a mean streak and wants his own way when he finds something that entices him."

"Well, it is not like I'm going to go all the way with this sting. I am just supposed to get him interested enough to try to commit the act of using his own sperm for the insemination. Well there," said Judith, "that takes care of that problem. In all seriousness Jac and Mike, how is this suppose to work? Getting him interested in me and into breaking the law should not be too hard. Am I going to be wired or something?"

"I will pick one of the newest bugs that can be worn on the clothes, and it looks like a piece of jewelry, which he won't notice. It is my impression that he is only into this for two reasons," said Mike. "First, putting up is finger to get revenge on his parentage, the inadequacy he must have felt from his mother's lack of attention and then too much. Second, his father's overpowering manner and overactive sexual glands that only led the doc into sexual trouble in his earlier years, and perhaps now, he, Calendar, subconsciously can't get enough sex either." Mike's voice trailed off as he started thinking about Frederick and the life he had been leading. Judith's voice brought him back for she was saying something. "I'm sorry, Judith, what did you say?"

Judith laughed and said, "Where were you? I asked you if there were any other reasons."

Mike laughed too and said, "Well, now that I think of it, there might be. His feeling of superiority as a genius makes him feel that he has the right to have his genes carried on long after he is gone. Final and the biggest reason is greed." Mike made the quote marks with his fingers as he spoke, "The *money*. I don't think I mentioned the amount of money he charges each couple. Two hundred thousand dollars for one insemination package, and often, it doesn't work the first time, so he gets another two hundred fifty thousand."

"Wow, pricewise, that kind of puts me out of the picture," said Judith.

"No, not really," said Jac. "He now knows that you have lots of friends who could afford it, and since you volunteered to help, I decided to open a trust account in your name for the sting, placing the amount of two hundred fifty thousand dollars into it from your recently deceased aunt Jubilee who lived in Alaska. I'm sure he will check you out before going forward with any action. If he asks any question about your aunt Jubilee, you can just tell him that she got her money from a plush entrepreneur company that she owned."

KaSandra looked at her watch and then said, "Oh, look at the time. You know your uncle doesn't like anyone coming in late for one of his functions, Jac, so we all better get going."

CHAPTER 19

At nine o'clock the next morning, after the big sting meeting at his godfather's home, Jac sat in his office, going over in his mind what the couples had said about their situations. All agreed that even though most of their children were now three to five years old, their origin does not make them less loved or wanted. Most of the men admitted that their child, not coming from their sperm, would take some time for them to adjust too. All couples also agree that for the amount of money they paid, there must be some justice done to correct the immoral and illegal act forced upon them by Dr. Calendar. Mr. Fiscal, speaking for the group, said, "Anything we can do as a group, just asks Mr. Castillo's staff to give me a call. They have my numbers. I'll then e-mail the rest." This was confirmed by all of the couples as they left to return to their lives.

"Justice, what does that mean?" said Jac out loud, shaking his head as if to clear out the reoccurring thoughts and again spoke, "What justice will there be for Kass? Even if we catch the doc red-handed with this sting, I don't think there will ever be enough justice." Looking at his watch, Jac realized that Judith should be arriving at the clinic right about now. She had made the appointment for ten o'clock that morning over a week ago after volunteering to be the bait.

CHAPTER 20

Judith had risen early to have plenty of time to get ready and to set the stage. She dressed meticulously in her navy blue suit with matching bag and shoes. Her only decorative pieces were small circle earrings and a borrowed plain circle pin from Mike for the lapel of her jacket. The pin was the recorder. She surveyed her reflection in the mirror and felt satisfied with her appearance. Checking her wristwatch for the third time, she noticed that it was seven and figured she had time for a cup of coffee and some pancakes with fresh raspberries—her favorite breakfast.

As she entered the restaurant, Jac waved her over to the table. She asked Peter to tell Joe that Judith was ready for her breakfast. The next half hour flew by as she ate, and Jac went over the basic details of her first meeting with Dr. Calendar again.

"Jac, do not worry so. I'm going to be all right. After all, I am sure we are only going to talk about the procedures today, and he will probably make another appointment for me. Mike figured he will take a few days to check me out, and so my second appointment well presumably be some time next week."

"I know, Judith. Your right, but I feel like I'm sending you into the lions den without even a whip to protect yourself." Judith laughed and placed her hand on top of Jac's, which was resting on the table not far from her.

"Jac, you worry too much. I have been briefed by Mike and you until I know what I am supposed to do backward and forward. Oh, as for a whip, I have these," and she held up her hand with their lovely fingers and even longer fingernails, "if he gets to frisky. There is one thing that you can do for me though."

"What? Name it and it's yours."

"Oh, careful there, Jac, I might take advantage of your offer." She laughed. "I would really like to take your car up to the clinic if you do not mind. Your fancy car can help, even if he has the license checked out." Without saying a word, Jac reached into his coat pocket and handed the car keys to Judith. And as he returned to his breakfast, he said, "Just remember that the code on the car phone for my cell here is star 449, and drive carefully." Judith got up, straightened her skirt, and took a few steps closer to Jac to kiss him on the cheek.

"Thanks for everything. I will not let you all down," Judith said as she walked away.

Judith barely noticed the drive up the coast for her mind was on how she was going to handle Dr. Calendar. She had been living the pampered life for almost a year now and was afraid that maybe she had lost her street smarts. To stay alive, she had never trusted anyone outside her family at face value. Now, living and working at the hotel with people who trusted and believed what she said was the truth, all that had changed for her. Being around KaSandra, Jac, Joe, and Mike, and her supervision of Crystal and Pete and their belief in her abilities helped her grow and accept her own values. "So what are you worrying about girl?" she asked herself as she maneuvered Jac's Porsche convertible up the highway. She started to relax as the warm inner coastal wind blew against her face. Licking her lips, she tasted salt water. Smiling at the reaction of her taste buds, she started to hum along with the CD.

Pulling up in front of the clinic, Judith checked her lipstick in the rearview mirror, and sighing deeply, she got out of the car. Looking around as she walked toward the front door, she noted for future reference that the parking lot had only three cars in it. This seemed strange for when she was here to help identify KaSandra after her disappearance, the lot was full of cars. Entering the office lobby, she was greeted by the receptionist with a cheer, "Good morning. May I help you?"

"Yes, I am Judith Polymer, and I have an appointment with Dr. Calendar."

"Oh, yes, Mrs. Polymer. The doctor will be right with you. While you are waiting, would you please fill out this registration form for our records?"

Judith smiled at the receptionist, who could not have been pass her twentieth birthday, and said, "Certainly, I would be very happy to fill in the registration, but I am Ms. Polymer, not Mrs." Taking the papers from the girl, Judith walked across the room to a set of white chairs and sat down.

As Judith sank into the cushion, the room became more visible to her. Maybe it was a reaction to the plush of the chair that drew her attention to the rest of her surroundings. There were four other chairs in the same style and fabric in the room, one love seat, and another sofa that faced a fireplace. These pieces of furniture were the same color as the walls, a lime green, and could have seated four adults comfortably; the other two chairs were just like the one she was sitting on. To finish the room, there were also four coffee tables with matching teak lamps on each. The shades of each lamp were in a soft cream that corresponded with the carpet, and an oriental rug of cream background with lime flowers patterned throughout in a design of lotus flowers. The walls were sparsely decorated with a few paisley wall arts of flowers colored in light pink, yellow, and green tones.

Across the room sat a couple who Judith would have guessed were in their early thirties. Watching them out of the corner of her eye, she noticed that they both seemed quite nervous. First, the man would get up and walk to the window and look out for a few minutes like he was searching for an answer. Then the woman would get up and join him at the window, and in low voices, which she could not hear, they would talk for a few minutes. Suddenly, both would walk back to their chairs and sit down again. She would fidget with her shirt, a cuff, or her pearls, and he would get up again to walk around the room. During all this, Judith started to wonder if they were going to be the doctor's next victims. Halfway through the forms, she heard the nurse say, "You're next Mr. and Mrs. Snead." The couple got up, and after looking at each other for reassurance, both followed the nurse out of the room.

Judith finished the forms with all the information memorized through hours of drilling from Mike and Jac. She mentioned all the places, schools, jobs, and relatives that had been worked out with precision beforehand. Not wanting to confront the youngster at the front desk again, Judith placed her information form down on the table next to her and picked up a copy of *Cosmopolitan*. She had gotten so interested in an article on "Sex and the Underworld" that she did not hear Dr. Calendar approach and stop a few feet in front of her. He stood there, studying her profile. Judith suddenly became aware that she was not alone and looked up, noticing her objective stand there, and upon eye contact, Frederick Calendar smiled and stated, "Well Ms. Polymer, have you finished those forms for me?"

Judith leaned forward and reached for the papers, and in doing so, she noticed that her skirt was showing far too much leg. Rising quickly and smiling back at Dr. Calendar, she handed him the forms and said, "Yes, I have finished and answered all of the questions correctly." She purposely spoke in a breath manner. As she said these words, she thought to herself, *How long were you standing there looking at me?*

"Oh, I'm sure they're just fine. Tell me, isn't it about lunchtime? Are you hungry, Ms. Judith? I hope you are not insulted by me using your first name. By the time we're finished here, I'm sure we will be quite familiar with each other."

Judith just stared at Frederick, stalling for some time to think and letting her eyes travel all over his face. Then she looked down at the clock on the table and said, "Oh, it certainly is lunchtime." Looking up at the reception desk, she noticed that there was no one at the desk, and it seemed suddenly too quiet in the office. Smiling back up at the doctor, she said, "Why yes, I believe I am getting quite hungry. I had such a little breakfast being so nervous and all."

"Ms. Judith, please don't be anxious. It is a very simple procedure, and anyway, by the time you're ready, everything will be quite clear to you on what we do here. Why don't you come back into the office area with me, and we will have some lunch and talk about getting you on the road to having a child of your own."

The phone's ringing brought Jac out of his reverie. He blinked once and pushed the speakerphone. "Hello," he said and was surprised to hear the voice on the other end.

"Hello, Jac, I thought I'd give you a call and let you know my decision on your offer," said Kaper. "Until you spend time behind bars, I see no reason to stop destroying what is near and dear to you."

"What do you mean? I haven't spent time behind bars?" Jac asked angrily. "I was in that position way before you were. If you recall, you framed me with that bogus real estate contract with my name and social security number on it. I was three days in jail before I could prove that the papers were phonies. I'd say, Kaper, that we are pretty even since it wasn't any of my scheming that gained you a prison term in the first place. So why don't you come down here, and I'll buy you dinner, then we can bury the hatchet. You know we are not kids anymore, and your father has been dead for months now." There was a long silence on the phone before Kaper Kalabrese spoke the words that Jac had been waiting to hear.

"Okay, Jac, I'll see you tomorrow night, but it's going to be one hell of a bill when I get finished with that dinner."

"Kap, stay a few days, and the whole tab will be on me. It will just be nice to see you and not worry that you're going to pull something. I'll see you tomorrow night here, right?"

"Yes, Jac, and thanks for making the offer to let bygones be bygones. See you soon." The phone went dead in Jac's hand, and he then realized that he had been holding his breath.

CHAPTER 21

Dr. Kay Sharon's voice brought KaSandra back from her daydream. She was thinking about the new life inside of her when the baby kicked, and she realized that she had not heard a word of what Kay was saying, "I'm sorry, Kay, what did you say? The baby just kicked me a good one, and I was concentrating on how strong it was." Dr. Sharon laughed and gave KaSandra belly a little pat.

"This little one is what I was talking about. You are doing very well, KaSandra, but I would like you to gain a few more pounds. The total weight that you have gained to date is just ten pounds, and you are in your seventh month. Ten pounds is not enough for this time frame. The baby is probably all right, but it is taking all of you nourishment, and if you catch even a cold, there might be some difficulties."

"I hear you, doctor, but I have such terrible heartburn that food just doesn't appeal to me, especially meat. All I like right now is celery and oranges."

"Try a little hot cereal, like oatmeal, maybe some creamed corn or potatoes. A malt or milk shake every day will help a lot in putting on some weight, and the ice cream has a lot of nutrition."

"Okay, I hear you, and I promise that I'll do my best," said KaSandra with a big smile as she headed toward the door.

"See that you do," said Dr. Sharon. "Or I'll notify that handsome man you work for and tell him you're not behaving." Dr. Kay, hoping Kass would tell Jac herself, heard KaSandra laughing to herself as she left the office. There were a few concerns about KaSandra's health that needed watching in all areas.

Judith smiled again at Dr. Calendar and followed him into the interior of the office. She noticed that she was walking down a hall that was decorated with paintings of the ocean and meadows that surrounded the clinic. Trying to sound calm, she asked, "Frederick did a local artist do the paintings?"

He laughed then said, "Yes, I guess you could say that. I did them myself. Do you like any one in particular?"

"Oh, that is hard to say. They all seem so special," she said.

Frederick laughed again as he opened a door that led the way into a very large room. "Thank you, Ms. Judith, for being so honest."

The room was accented in the same style as the lobby. It had green walls and cream-colored drapes. The carpet with a green design was the same as the front room. The drapes were moving slightly from the wind coming off the ocean. Behind the sheer drapes were glass doors that covered the full length of the wall that leads out to a very large patio. Judith looked around the room and noticed a very large teak desk with two very comfortable-looking chairs sitting in front of it, slightly slanted to the angle of the desk.

The wall had hangings that were in an Asian motif. Dr. Calendar walked over to his desk and spoke into the intercom, saying, "Charles, you can proceed with the serving of lunch now. The patio, Ms. Judith." Frederick gestured. "We will be dining out there, and I hope you don't mind a little soft breeze."

Looking through the doors, Judith saw some men carrying silver trays toward a table covered in a white tablecloth. "Do you treat all your perspective patients this way, Dr. Calendar?"

"Frederick, please, Judith. Now to answer your question, when I saw that you were coming up to the clinic for a consultation, well…" He hesitated, and looking at her, he said, "Let me be frank. You must have seen that last time you were up here that I had a very keen interest in you."

He offered his arm to lead her outside. Judith ignored his statement and placed her hand through his curved arm. As they walked out to the table, which was now ready for their lunch, she noticed the luxury of the table settings. On top of the white linen tablecloth were two sterling flatware place settings, each handle set in gold. The glassware looked like the Waterford that she had just seen in one of the dream catalogs that arrived at the hotel. The centerpieces were pink-tinged orchids, floating in a crystal bowl. On her pink napkin, which matched the centerpieces, was an enormous white orchid. Frederick pulled out her chair and motioned for her to sit down.

As she took her chair, she noticed that her heart was beating so loud in her ears that she was sure he could hear it. She knew this was not good, so she tried to calm herself and think about what an amoral man he was.

Her heartbeat started to quiet as she noticed that he was asking her if she liked lobster. He continued with his speech as if she had answered and mentioned how he had the lobster flown in from Miami just that morning. One of the men that had set the table appeared and started pouring white wine into the crystal goblet in front of her. She reached for her napkin, trying to think of something to say, something that would defuse the situation a little.

"Doctor, ah…" She hesitated. "Frederick, this is all very gracious of you." She spread her hand up to include the table. "But I think we should be talking about the reason I am here."

"A lady that gets right to the point. I like that. I do think, Ms. Judith, that we can do both on such a lovely day as this, don't you? Come now, help yourself to some of this delectable food, and we will discuss the procedure as you wish."

Frederick looked at Judith more sternly and said, "I hope you don't mind, but I had you investigated. I am a businessman who cannot afford to be careless nowadays. I received information from my sources at a financial establishment that you have come into a considerable amount of money recently."

"You do not surprise me. I knew you would check. That money you found out about was an inheritance from my aunt Jubilee who died recently in Alaska. Without that money, I would not be able to fulfill one of my strongest desires. I had mentioned longing to have a child without being married to my aunt several years ago, and I guess she remembered." *There*, thought Judith as she reached for the salad spoon that was delivered with just enough emphasis. *And I did not go over board.*

"Tell me, didn't your aunt…ah, did you mention her name? Oh, no matter. Didn't she seem surprised that you wanted a baby without the convenience of a marriage certificate?"

Judith laughed then said, "Not my aunt Jubilee. My other aunts maybe, but not my father's sister." Judith knew that she had to keep the questions in her court so Frederick would not get suspicious. Taking a sip of water, she started to say, "So you see—"

"Excuse me, but is not the wine to your liking?" asked Frederick.

"It is just fine. I wanted to clear my taste buds before savoring the banquet again. Tell me, Frederick," Judith continued as she reached for her wineglass and took a very small sip so she can keep her mind clear, "I understand that I can bring in a sperm sample from a donor. Is that correct?" Frederick coughed on a piece of lobster as he heared Judith's direct question.

"Yes, that is correct, or you can allow me to work with my people in the business and save yourself some inconvenience."

"Oh, how do you do that? Do I not have to pick a donor out of a book or something? The type of man that I want to be the donor?"

"No, you just give me an itemized description of the type of man you want. You know, his looks, education, ethnic background, etc. Those kinds of details."

Judith thought, *Boy you sure do not waste time on getting the person into your method of thinking.* "Oh, I have all my requirements written down on a list that I gave the sperm bank in Miami when I decided to do this a couple of years ago. Could you just get the list from them?"

Frederick thought, *That is just what I need, some outside agency poking their nose into my business.* "Yes, you can just give me the agency's name, and I'll get my people at the bank to contact them and save you a trip to Miami, unless you were going for some other reason. I know you young women who live so far from the big metropolis love to get up there now and then."

"Oh, that will be just great," Judith stated as she took a small bite out of a cherry dipped in whipped cream. "Frederick, can you tell me a little about how we proceed after the donor's specimen is in the clinic?"

"Ms. Judith, if you are finished with your cherry, I can show you better than I can explain. Let me take you into the part of the clinic were the procedure is done and show you how the system works. Then I will have my assistant set you up for an examination next week at your convenience."

CHAPTER 22

Jac had just sat down in is favorite spot, overlooking the ocean for a late lunch when Kass walked up carrying a pineapple malt milkshake that Joe had just made for her. "Wow," said Jac. "That looks good, and I don't even think I've had one." Kass sat down and place the malt on the table, saying, "Well, you can have this one for I'm not really hungry. I only ordered it because Dr. Sharon said I have to gain weight, and every time I eat something, I get a terrible heartburn, which it's not worth the trouble."

"Well, can the doctor give you something for the pain?" asked Jac. "Oh, I am already taking Phillips, but that doesn't help me gain weight. Kay said that if I get a cold that I would not have much to fight it off with for the baby is taking all the nourishment from me," said Kass.

"Well, there must be something I can do to help. Do you want me to talk to your doctor?" asked Jac.

Kass was silent for quite a long time and finally said, "Well, two heads are better than one, and I'm at the end of my strength over this problem." Kass reached over and took Jac's pen from his shirt pocket, and on a napkin, she wrote down her doctor's number and handed it to Jac. She said, "Here, Jac, is my doctor's number, Dr. Kay Sharon. When you get her, just tell her that you have my permission to talk to her and she can relate anything she wants about my pregnancy."

After his caesar salad and iced tea, Jac called and talked for thirty minutes with Kass's doctor, Kay Sharon. Dr. Sharon had related her concerns about some abnormalities in some of the tests she had Kass take. She also stated, "There is no dire emergency as of yet, but I'm concerned. I would like to make you aware of a few problems that might arise in KaSandra's pregnancy."

"Yes, of course, doctor. Please continue," said Jac.

"Well, Mr. Scarin, KaSandra is not gaining weight the way she should be. I have talked to her about this, and she's promise to eat more. I know that she is having trouble keeping food in her stomach, and I've suggested some foods that are soft and easy to digest. Then there is the problem of her blood pressure. It tends to be a little high, and this is another concern. If it doesn't settle down, we may have to take the baby early. KaSandra has a genetic link with toxemia that can occur in first pregnancies of women near thirty-five. Mr. Scarin, I have asked her to only work half a day and rest in some shaded cool spot during the heat of the day. Do you think you can help me with this matter?"

Jac had been listening very intently as the doctor was talking and had wished that Kass had come to him about these concerns earlier. "Yes, Dr. Sharon, I would be happy to assist you in keeping Kass and the baby healthy. There should be no problem with her working only half days. Furthermore, I would like a number that I can reach you or someone on your staff in case something does happen, if that is all right."

"Certainly, Mr. Scarin. My office number is 456-1000, and my pager is 1-800-456-2000. Mr. Scarin, KaSandra is a healthy woman, and this pregnancy of hers is going well for it being a first baby and her age. I'm just glad someone will be there to help her."

"Doctor, I really appreciate you talking to me. Kass is very special to me. You see, I've known her since we were kids in school in New York. I will also alert the rest of my staff to your number in case I am on business."

Jac was so deep in thought about Kass's problem that he did not see her approach. "Peter, will you please bring Jac a glass of white wine from private stock and a glass of fruit juice for me," said Kass to the bartender as she crossed the room toward Jac, who was sitting with a very serious look on his face.

"What is wrong with you, Jac? Is everything alright? You should see your face."

Jac was surprised out of is reverie by Kass's voice but didn't want to go into what he had been thinking about so he prevaricated. "I'm a little concerned as Judith is not back yet."

"What time was her appointment with Dr. Calendar?" asked Kass as she took the seat across from Jac.

"The appointment was at eleven, and it is now well after three," said Peter, overhearing Kass's question as he set the two drinks down on the table. Kass took a long sip of her fruit juice and looked up after setting the glass down. She smiled and said, "Well, I guess you can stop worrying, Jac and Peter, for here she comes now."

Judith was walking across the beach, carrying her shoes and wearing on her shoulder the white orchid that had adorned her napkin. She had driven Jac's car back and parked it in his spot then walked down to the beach to think over what had transpired in the last four hours. Spying her three friends watching her approach, she waved and crossed the sand in front of the hotel.

"That must have been some first contact. You have been gone for four hours," said Jac.

"Oh," said Judith, smiling a weak smile. "The doctor treated me to lunch on a patio that overlooks the ocean, and then we took a tour of the clinic where he does his procedures. I am expected to go back next Wednesday for an examination, and Frederick said I should bring my list of details on what kind of sperm donor I require."

"Frederick, lunch, and an orchid. Weren't you supposed to be getting information on how we could trap this man? Not fall for him," said KaSandra.

"Calm yourself, girl. I could not refuse his hospitality without getting him suspicious, could I? I got the information we needed on the recorder..." She pointed to the pin. "By letting him think I was on the level and wanted a baby. The tour was real helpful. I found out that there are two areas of files in the offices, and I saw the obvious ones behind the reception desk with all the names and addresses and then some in his private office."

"How did you get into his private office?" asked Jac.

"I really did not get into the office. He got a phone call during our tour and excused himself to answer it, leaving me alone in the surgery. I followed him to the room where he was talking on the phone. I could see in even though I am sure he thought he had closed the door. I was close enough to spy through the door crack and saw four more file cabinets against the southeast wall. I also heard him say to someone that they had to go through with the surgery that week. The sperm was already in the clinic, and he had scheduled the time for the transfer. They must have said something back that really irritated him for he came out of the office all red and wiping his face. I thought you could freeze sperm for an indefinite length of time," said Judith.

"It sure would be wonderful if we know who he was talking to and see if they canceled for a particular reason," said KaSandra.

"Mike did it before and got the phone numbers of the people the doctor had swindled, so maybe he could do it again. I'll ask him," said Jac.

"Now, all we have to figure out is how we are going to get into his office and into those files," said Judith.

"It would be helpful to know how many times he had used his own sperm and on which client files, but it would not be permissible in a court of law without a search warrant, let alone the confidentiality issue," said KaSandra.

"So what do we do next, boss?" asked Judith.

"Well, I don't think he will do anything to you on the first examination. He probably thinks he needs more time to get your confidence, and a man like this doesn't want to rush anything. The chase is half his fun, and of course, you will have to be physically ready to ovulate for him to be sure that his sperm will create another baby for him. You are pretty safe going to that appointment next Wednesday, I hope," said Jac.

"Well, I better get Mike on the phone and see if he can find out who was on the other end of that conversation you heard before next Wednesday, just in case. They may have been canceling an in vitro fertilization procedure, and he has already stored his sperm in the petri dish. By the way, where is my car?"

"Why, in your parking space where I parked it," said Judith with a smile.

That night, Judith laid awake, wondering what she had gotten herself into. If what Jac had said was correct and Frederick had already retrieved his sperm, he might ask her if he could take her eggs during the examination. What would she do then? If she refused, he would be suspicious of her motives, but she figured that though that might be the best way to proceed, nothing would happen to her until he tried to place them both back into her body, and then they would have him.

CHAPTER 23

Frederick sat with his feet up on his desk. His last patient of the day had just left, and he had time to think about Judith Polymer. He didn't think he would have such a strong reaction to her as he had that afternoon. He had remembered how he felt when he first shook her hand when she came with the others to pick up KaSandra four months ago. KaSandra had been lovely with her fair and creamy body, and the baby that comes from their union will be just as fair and lovely.

Then there is that ebony skin of Judith with those high French-looking cheek bones and very long face. *The slight slant of those dark eyes as she looked at me,* he thought, *and the way she wears her wild hair all back behind her ears and then looking so very full behind her head.*

I sure wish I could have seen the rest of the pink slip she was wearing. I'm sure she would have been very self-conscious if she knew that I saw the lace and brown skin peeking from under her nice-fitting suit. I actually think she blushed a little when she saw the luncheon table and the orchid that I chose for her. Oh! How could I forget that red tongue of hers that she so often fluttered across her lips as she savored the food, especially the cherries?

Yes, I'm going to savor the time I have with her. Every since I first saw her, I could feel my skin quiver and my groin go all wet just like it is doing now. When she is under the sodium pentothal, I wonder if I should just impregnate her right then instead of removing her eggs.

No, take the eggs also, Frederick. You can have two babies from this blending. Two very special babies, he thought. *I can tell.*

After Judith's visit with Calendar, KaSandra sat looking out at the ocean, sipping at a fruit juice and waiting for her lunch. *I wonder if I'll be able to keep this lunch down,* she thought. *Dr. Kay told me that I've got to gain some weight, at least ten pounds, but every time I eat, it just comes right up. The only thing I seem to keep down is celery, oranges, oatmeal, and I'm hoping the chicken slices that I'm having for lunch.* "Only two months left, little one," KaSandra said to her stomach.

Joe appeared from the kitchen and set a beautiful plate of food in front of her: two slices of boiled chicken, several sticks of celery, and sliced oranges sitting on cottage cheese. "Oh, now that I see the food, I feel sick again," said KaSandra to herself. "That really looks good. Thanks, Joe."

Joe smiled and turned to walk back to the kitchen. Spying Jac as he walked through the restaurant doors, he stopped and waited for him to catch up. "Boss, I just served KaSandra some lunch, but I get the feeling that most of it will come back to the kitchen untouched."

Jac looked across the room to where Kass sat with her back to him. "What did you bring her, Joe?"

"Just a lot of soft food. Celery, oranges, cottage cheese, and a couple slices of chicken. Those are about the only things she seems to be able to keep down nowadays."

"Mmmm…Sounds good. Why not bring me the same, and add several slices of toast with jam. Maybe if I eat with her and keep her mind off what she's eating, the food will stay where it's supposed to, and she'll gain some weight."

Jac patted Joe on the shoulder and walked over to the table where Kass still sat not touching the food. "Hi there, little mama, how are we doing today? That food looked so good I asked Joe to serve me the same."

Kass looked up at Jac and smiled. "What, changing the hour of your usual lunch today? What a surprise, Jac."

"All right, cut the sarcasm, and invite me to eat with you."

Jac had left Kass at her door after their lunch together, and she promised to put her feet up and rest. She had eaten everything that was put in front of her plus several slices of toast that Jac had in front of him. Maybe, just maybe, she will keep this food down and gain an ounce or two. *I must remember to ask Joe to work on some kind of shake or malt that will be full of nutrition and protein to help Kass gain even more weight.* As he reached his office door, he could hear the phone ringing and quickened his pace to the desk. "Hello, Jac here."

"Jac, this is Kaper, and I'm calling to tell you that I won't be partaking of food with you ever. In fact, I would prefer not ever seeing you again in this lifetime. Oh, don't worry. I'm stopping the pranks for you're right about something, my father being dead for almost a year, and I should get over what he used to do to me. But that's not so easy, old friend. It didn't happen to you, but not to worry, this is the last time you will hear my voice. I am sending you something in the mail that will finish this situation once and for all. Good-bye, Jac," and the phone went dead before Jac could even say a word.

"What's up my friend? It looks like you just got bad news from the expression on your face," said Mike.

Jac looked up at Mike, and after placing the handle of the phone back, he said, "That was Kaper, and he's sending me something in the mail that will finish the pranks forever. He doesn't ever want to see or hear from me again."

"Well, that sounds like a threat. What is he sending?" asked Mike.

"That's just it. I don't know. He didn't stay on the phone long enough for me to ask him," Jac replied.

"Well, I think you better take your mail for the next few weeks over to the hospital and have it x-rayed before you open any of it," said Mike.

"Oh, I don't think he wants me dead for he probably would have done that a long time ago. He had plenty of chances. No, I think this mystery of why he dislikes me so much will finally be solved. Well, anyway, Mike, I'm glad you're here for I was going to call you."

"Judith told Kass and me after she got back from her first appointment with Dr. Calendar that he got a very interesting phone call from someone yesterday. I was wondering if you could contact the friend who helped you before and see if they can get a name on the phone call that came in while Judith was at the clinic, about twelve o'clock or so. They were canceling their appointment for insemination."

"Sure, that's no problem. It gives me a reason to see her again," said Mike with a grin. "There is a bit of news from your uncle though. He said he tried to get you without luck and so called me. It seems that our six couples have been keeping in touch with each other and have decided to check the blood type of all their adopted children. They are going to learn if there is any possible connection among their children and then match it with Dr. Calendar's blood or DNA. Your uncle said he would be very willing to get the good doctor's blood for the test. If you are not too busy, he would like you to call him about the probability."

Mike had finished the sentence with a great big smile on his face, which made Jac think he knew more than he was saying. "What's going on? You look like the mouse that got the cheese from the trap."

"Oh, nothing so grand. I was just picturing your uncle getting that blood or DNA from the doctor and how he would do it. You obviously don't want your uncle to get the evidence, so how are you going to? Any thoughts?"

"Not at the moment," Jac said. "I will call Tony even though that means another visit to his home, which I would rather not do." Jac's mind drifted back to the last visit with his uncle, and a chill went over his body. He loves that man of steel, but his methods were a little too old fashioned for today's society. Or were they? And he shivered again.

Mike had been watching Jac and saw the shiver that spread over his body. It made him wonder what hold Tony had on Jac. Was he really afraid of his uncle? Mike thought the man is quite intriguing in that old Italian family sort of way. Mike, shortly after meeting Tony, did a little investigating on him and found out some very interesting material. He was still inside the law in his business dealings—but barely—and that was for him to know, as far as the police were concerned, for Mike wasn't part of the police force anymore.

"So, Jac, what is our next move? I presume that Judith is going for another visit to the doctor's office in the near future, which will probably get the doctor's program in motion. How far is she willing to go with this charade? I understand that the procedure of getting the eggs out is quite painful, and she really doesn't want a baby that way, does she? After all, we already have one female friend going through the program against her will. *Right?*"

Jac nodded his head in affirmative and started to fill Mike in on what the plans were when suddenly there was a rap at his door. Crystal poked her head in the door and said, "Jac, there is a special delivery for you at the desk, and the delivery person said he can only put it into your hands."

CHAPTER 24

Jac proceeded out to the reception, and on seeing the delivery person, he said, "Hi, I'm Jac Scarin, and I was told you have a package for me?"

"Yes, sir," said the rather shy young man holding a package about the size of a shoe box. "I was also told to ask you for some ID before turning this over." Jac nodded and reached into his pocket for his wallet. Fishing out his driver's license, he handed it to the driver, at the same time forcing a smile.

After the driver checked his picture on the license, he handed Jac a piece of paper and asked for his signature. Taking the paper, Jac scribbled his name and handed it back, taking hold of the box with his other hand. He smiled again, saying, "Thanks."

The driver saw that Jac had laid a ten-dollar bill on top of the paper, and his face lit up. "Wow. Thanks, mister! Hope I can come here again."

Mike, who had been leaning against the lobby counter, started to laugh. "So, Jac, what's in the box that you had to show ID for?"

Hearing Mike's comment, the driver who was leaving, stopped and said, "It must be awful important for he instructed me to give it only to Jac Scarin."

"What is his name?" Mike asked as the smile left his face.

The driver, still standing by the open door of the hotel and thinking that Mike was talking to him, looked at Mike and said, "Well, I don't know his name, but he sure was dressed well with that linen suit and all. I'd swear…" the driver said, shaking his head, "it was a silk shirt and tie. Real fancy this guy and not from down here."

"Why not from down here?" Mike was just curious to see if it really was Kaper who gave the package in person.

The driver looked pleased to be still part of this mystery package, which he had shaken and searched for an opening in the brown tape just to get just some idea of its contents before he made the delivery. "Well, he had this different kind of accent. I bet he was a Northerner. He was tall, about your height, Mr. Scarin, but blond with blue eyes. Oh yeah, he had a scar right down the side of his face from below the eye to under his jawbone. Otherwise, I'd say a good-looking dude. Thanks again for the ten."

"Kaper." Mike and Jac both said at the same time. Jac immediately turned and headed for his office. "Wait, Jac," Mike said, running after him, "you don't know what is in that box. You shouldn't open it until we have it checked."

"Mike, it's all right. Didn't you see the way that driver looked at the box as you were questioning him? I'm sure he's shook it and tried everything under the sun to see what is in here." As Jac finished talking, he lifted the lid off the shoe box and revealed a large cassette.

"One black VHS tape is all it contains. No note or other hidden messages?" was all Mike could manage to say. Jac laughed and removed the tape, heading toward the VCR. "What did you expect, a boom?"

Slipping the black box into the opening, the machine came alive as the tape opened up on the face of Kaper smiling back at them. Seeing his mouth move, Jac adjusted the volume and heard him say, "Hi, old friend, if you are listening to this tape, I am down here with the fallen angels, waiting for you."

Jac couldn't conceal his surprise as he looked at the face of his boyhood friend. Kaper had changed so much since Jac had seen him at his mother's funeral. Kaper had been gaunt and moody then. Jac had contributed that to just getting out of prison on early release when the fire inspector finally stated that it was an accidental fire. Another charge the feds were trying to pin on him.

Jac had never asked but presumed that a lot of money had changed hands just to get an early release so he could go home for his mother's funeral. After all, he wasn't a killer or a bank robber. He just didn't pay all his taxes. Jac also noted then that Kaper and his father were not standing together at the church or gravesite. Jac had hoped that they had made up their differences for the two of them were all the family they had left.

Kaper's voice brought Jac back to reality. He stopped the tape and reversed to repeat what he had said.

"Jac take a good look at what your handy work has done to me."

Kaper slowly turned his head to the left to reveal the right side of his face. There was the scar that the driver had revealed in his description.

Then Jac heard that hideous laughter. The same laugh he had heard the last time he had talked with Kaper on the phone.

"Yes, you are to blame for this and much more after my *father dearest* saw you at the funeral of my mother. Saw how successful you looked and heard from others how great you were doing in Key West, he started in on me again. This time I fought back, and he had some of his so-called friend do this to me."

Jac saw Kaper's hand rub over the scar and then heard that same awful maniac laughter.

"Did you know, Jac, that they still haven't figured out what killed him? His picture that hung on the wall behind his desk revealed a slash down his face but other than that, not a mark on him. The police harassed me right away, but I had the best of alibis. I was still recovering from Father's handiwork in the hospital."

I have left a few clues that lead in your direction for by the time you see this, I will have disappeared and presumed possible death. But I'm not worried. With your connections, you'll have nothing to worry about. I'm sorry to say you were luckier in your kin than I.

"Oh, Jac, father's will was read a couple of months ago, and he left everything to charity, except for some reason, you were mentioned, and his attorneys couldn't find you for the reading. I wonder why."

"Jac, old friend, have fun explaining these circumstances to the police when they come to call. I don't really want to leave them any extra clues, so this tape will self-destruct after my last sentence. Good-bye, and see you in hell."

Jac and Mike heard that terrible laughter again, and Mike quickly ejected the tape out of the machine and drowned it with water.

Laughter still echoed in Jac ears as he sat there, staring at the blank screen. "Sick. I can't believe how sick he was."

"That is if he is dead like he wants you to believe," said Mike.

"I think the first thing I should do is check and see if Kaper's father is really dead, and if so, how he died," Mike said. "Then I'm going to check on Kaper and see if there is a death notice on him, and who's the last person who saw him preferably alive after the delivery person," said Mike as Jac started to leave the office then stopped. "Where are you going to start looking? Syracuse, right? The family mausoleum is located in St. Patrick's cemetery in Syracuse. I'm sure the family would have buried him with the other Kalabreses. Then maybe check out the New York City resident where the senior Kalabrese lived." Jac said.

"Who's left to bury him? I thought Kaper was the last of the line," said Mike.

"Yes, Kaper was the last male, but his father had some sisters, and they're still living on the homestead and in their late 80s," said Jac.

"So I'm off to Syracuse, but I might as well check out the family attorney Kaper mentioned while I'm in New York and see what that is all about. Do you mind if I use your phone to call that friend at the telephone company to get the last call on Calendar's phone? And where are you off to in such a hurry?" asked Mike. "Oh, I promised Tony I'd stop by an hour ago, and now I late. Help yourself, and have a good flight, Mike," said Jac as he left the office.

As mike settled down in Jac's chair to make some calls, he heard a crash and a terrible cry and saw KaSandra standing in her office door, holding her stomach.

"My water just broke," she exclaimed.

Mike reacted right after hearing KaSandra's cry. "Crystal, call Dr. Kay Sharon to tell her that KaSandra's baby is coming and I'm taking her to the hospital. Second, call the hospital and tell them in emergency that a pregnant mother is on her way in and that her water has broken."

"Mike," Crystal started to say, "this is KaSandra's first baby, and if she is not in labor, it might be hours before the baby gets here."

"Crystal, you are most likely right, but I'm not taking any chances since her water broke. I'm taking KaSandra to the hospital. Call Jac on his phone, and let him know what is happening. I hope we make it," said Mike.

Before Mike had finished his sentence, he helped KaSandra out the door of the hotel and toward his car. KaSandra bit her lip not to scream out as she was standing at the curb, waiting. "Mike," KaSandra moaned, "I don't think I'm going to make it to the hospital. I can feel the baby crowning right now."

"Good grief! How long have you been in labor?" Mike said as he ran back toward her.

"Oh, about an hour, but it wasn't too bad until after the water broke. That must have really started something." Mike changed their direction and went back into the hotel. He stopped just long enough to pick KaSandra up before going through the open door being held by Crystal.

"What now?" Crystal asked as she saw Mike running back into the hotel and over to the open elevator.

"Crystal, call all those people back. Start with the doctor, and tell them we are not going to make the hospital, and if they don't hurry, the baby will be here without them," said Mike as the elevator door closed.

As they got out on the second floor, Mike raced down the hall to KaSandra's room and just about kicked the door down before going through it. KaSandra let out another half moan, half scream as she was laid on her bed. "Mike, we have never been close friends, but if you get me through this, expect to be the godfather."

Before she could say anything more, Mike removed her undergarments and ran to the bathroom for towels. Then he heard a full scream from the mother-to-be as he returned to the outer room. "Boy! This baby doesn't want to wait for anyone, does he?"

"What makes you think it's a boy?" KaSandra said through her clenched teeth.

"What?" said Mike, laughing. "A girl has more self-respect to come into the world in a rush." As he squatted down at the end of the bed to see how far the baby was protruding, Mike had just enough time to stretch out his arms and catch the baby as KaSandra gave out another high-pitched scream and pushed her baby into the world.

"Well, it's a boy alright, and he looks real healthy," Mike said. He patted the boy on his bottom to start him crying, then wrapped the baby in the towel he had brought from the bathroom.

While all this was going on Jac, Judith, and Crystal arrived and were standing very quietly at the door, taking in a very beautiful scene. Jac would never have anticipated that Mike could be so gentle and graceful for such a big man. Watching him deliver the baby, wrap him in the towel, and hand him to his mother was one of the greatest experiences Jac's had in his life. Jac had known that Mike had delivered many of the babies in the Keys for many of the natives could not afford to go to the hospital. With doctors, and even midwives, in limited demand, the local police filled in many a time as the mother's delivery person. *So why am I having such a reaction to seeing Mike deliver Kass's baby?* Jac thought as Mike covered Kass to give her, her modesty and privacy.

KaSandra lay quite, watching her baby after the quickness of her delivery. With Mike taking care of the baby, Kass had to smile at his quick and disciplined movements. Then a sharp moan caught Mike's attention, and he placed the baby at the bottom of the bed as the pains of the afterbirth started. Mike smiled and said, "KaSandra, a few quick breaths and push." Then gently after he finished with her again, he covered her and directed his attention back to the baby. It had all lasted about thirty minutes, and from the looks of the room, you'd never guess that she had just delivered a five-pound-four-ounced baby boy.

"Well, don't just stand there with those stupid looks on your faces. Come on in, and take a look at this beautiful boy, if that's what you can call a baby boy," said Mike as he beamed with pride at the glow and beauty he saw looking down at KaSandra laying there, holding her son.

All stood around, looking down at the baby, trying to outdo each other with well wishes and congratulations when they where interrupted by Dr. Sharon as she rushed into the room, only to find she was too late.

"Well, isn't this a happy scene? But the mother and baby should be given some space, and please let me in so I can examine my patient. Now out, all of you, and tell the ambulance driver to wait awhile in case KaSandra needs to be moved to the hospital."

As the door closed on that happy scene, Jac could not help thinking how extraordinary the whole occurrence had been. He found that his thoughts on his marital status and the feelings about becoming a father to that little bundle of joy in the room were changing.

KaSandra was not sure how she was feeling at that moment for everything had moved so fast. The last thing she remembered fully was watching Mike take care of her son and then laying him in her arms. Shortly before that, she remembered she had walked out of the hotel in quite a lot of pain, knowing she was about to become a mother.

Mike had been so appropriate, she mused the way he had taken over the situation and given orders. *When had he carried me upstairs and placed me on the bed? It must had been just as I felt the baby's head coming out, but he caught him and cared for him in such a remarkably gentle way. I never once felt embarrassed in his presence, and his confidence was reassuring. I'm sure glad he was in the hotel when my water broke. Seeing my friends' happy faces all around me, talking and smiling down at me and the baby, why was I afraid they would have looked down on me for having this phenomenal baby, lying here in my arms? Why had I been so afraid to bring this baby into this happy group of people? He will have nothing but love, strength, guidance, and happiness just the way I have had the last few years among all of them.*

"KaSandra. KaSandra. Hey, come on back and talk to me, girl. How are you feeling?" She finally heard Dr. Sharon asking her.

"Oh, Kay, I am in so much joy. I never knew I could feel this way, and just look at this precious baby here, and he's mine."

"Yes, he seems to be in excellent condition. A little small, but his lungs are clear and heart is strong and so well taken cared of, but that doesn't surprise me for I've run into Mike and his work before. If it wasn't for the people like Mike and the police here in the Keys, we might have lost a lot of our babies over the years." After examining her, Kay said, "KaSandra, you also look fine, but I would feel better if you spent some time in the hospital where I can keep you under observation for a few days more."

"No, I feel fine, and I have a whole hotel full of friends that won't let me do a thing for weeks I'm sure. Just say I can stay here, and I'll be very good. I promise."

"Well, alright, but in bed as much as possible, and no stairs. I will also be telling Jac and the others that you are suppose to be quite and rest for two to three weeks before doing any work for this hotel. Do you hear me?" Kay looked down at the happy sight below her and smiled, not expecting an answer for both of her patients were occupied in each other.

"Yes, Kay, and thanks for giving into me and the baby."

"Okay. Now rest," said Dr. Sharon as she started to get up.

"By the way, since I have to make out a birth certificate for our newest arrival, what are you going to call him?"

KaSandra smiled a very wicked smile and said, "Jac Michael Cassillian, after the man I hope will be his father and the man who brought him into the world. I think both of them will be a strong influence on his life, and that is strictly between the two of us for I still don't know how I'm going to get Jac to marry me."

"Hey, I resent that. I thought you knew the law and me better than that. You know, doctor-patient confidentiality and all that? My lips are sealed for everything except his name. Get some sleep now."

The last thing KaSandra heard was the click of the door and the soft sounds coming from her new son as she drifted off to sleep, feeling quite pleased with herself.

CHAPTER 25

Jac couldn't help himself after listening to Dr. Sharon for about half an hour on how serious it was that Kass gets her strength back and gain a little weight. He quietly opened Kass's door to see if she was awake. He found her still asleep and was not surprised after the great job she had done earlier. He stood there for quite a long time before deciding to pick up the boy and hold him.

Jac had never held a baby before, especially one so small. Still standing and wanting to check this little one out further, he walked over to the rocking chair and sat down. Slowly he unwrapped the baby's blanket, trying not to get the baby too cold and looked at his little hands and feet. He found himself counting the toes, touching each one as he did. The feet weren't as big as his small finger and were oh so pink. As Jac was looking at the baby's hands, he noticed that the baby's eyes were open and wondered if he could see yet. The eyes were such a deep cobalt blue that Jac was sure they would always stay that way, just the same color of Kass.

Jac's head was bent over the baby when Kass awoke and felt for her son. Not finding him, she opened her eyes and saw Jac with the baby on his lap, inspecting his little body and smiling. Kass couldn't help smiling to herself and realized that it might not be too hard to get Jac to marry her if this was his reaction to a baby who wasn't even his. She saw that he straightened up, so she closed her eyes again, not wanting to disturb what she was watching. Through her lashes, she saw Jac stand up with the baby cradled in his arm. She watched him as he walked up and down, softly cooing. Kass realized that the baby must have been awake and Jac didn't want him to cry and wake her. Suddenly, Jac stopped walking and turned toward the bed. Seeing that Kass was awake, he walked over to the bed and set the baby down, whispering, "I think he is hungry."

Kass had decided to breast-feed a long time ago but was not quite sure she remembered all the nurse's instruction that she had received at the nursing class. Jac, realizing that she was nervous, started to help her to sit up and propped an extra pillow behind her for support.

"I'm not sure if I remember how," said Kass.

"Do you want me to go and get Crystal? She's had several children and might know what you are supposed to do." said Jac.

"No, wait a minute, Jac, and let's see if little Jac will just take my nipple by himself."

Carefully, Kass placed her nipple in the baby's mouth and held back the rest of her breast with her fingers. The baby didn't do anything at first, and then all of a sudden, he clamped on and started moving his mouth in a sucking motion.

"I'm not sure there is any milk for him to get yet. Dr. Kay said it might be a day or so."

"Well, he seems pretty content, and so do you, so something must be working all right. Say, did I hear you call him Jac?"

"Yes, didn't Dr. Kay tell you all his names?" asked Kass.

"What names?"

"I named him Jac Michael Cassillian after you and Mike for all the help you two have given me over the last seven months. I hope that's all right with you."

"I'm thrilled that you named him after me, and I'm sure Mike will be also." At that, Jac walked over to the rocker. He picked it up, strolled back to the bed, and sat down to watch Kass and her baby. He couldn't make himself leave just yet.

After the excitement of the morning, Mike was ready to hear the news about the person on the other end of the telephone call Judith overheard while at the clinic. Crystal had called him in the restaurant to inform him that there was a phone call for him in Jac's office. He had put a call to his friend at the telephone company earlier, asking her if she could help a lot of people out by finding the number and possible name of the caller who called Dr. Calendar's office around noon last Wednesday. She was returning his call; he hoped picking up the phone was good news.

"Hello, Maggie, what do you have for me?"

"Mike, you owe me big time," came the purr across the receiver, and Mike smiled to himself.

"Now, Maggie, you know I'm good for it. What did you find out?"

"Hold on to that thought. The call came from the governor's mansion in Tallahassee. What are you into now, Mike, that you are investigating the governor?"

"Not investigating. Just trying to save someone from some real bad pain."

"Well, if you can save the governor some pain, you would be in solid for the next four to eight years."

"Maggie, my beauty, I do owe you. Give me a couple of days, and the two of us will go out for dinner. Your choice."

"Mike, you've got it. If you don't call me, I will call you to collect. Bye for now."

As Mike replaced the receiver, he smiled at the thought of Maggie and those tight dresses she loved to wear to get her men friends hot and bothered. And it worked. He didn't notice Judith standing in the door of Jac's office, and when she spoke, he jumped.

"My, that must have been some phone call that it makes you so jumpy," she said with a hint of sarcasm in her voice. "Was it good news, Mike?"

"Yes, and if you take that look off your face, I will tell you about it. Do you know where Jac is?"

"The last time I saw him, he was holding KaSandra's baby and rocking it back and forth while he cooed to him. Boy, is he a goner, and I'm very surprised."

"Oh, why, I always thought Jac would have made a good father and wondered why he wasn't married a long time ago. You know Italian blood, family feelings about children, and all?"

CHAPTER 26

"Mike, do you think—" Judith was about to say as Jac walked through the door of his office and asked, "Think what, Judith?"

"Think I should go and look for you. Mike just got some important information on that mysterious phone call I overheard at Dr. Calendar's office last week."

Jac pulled his chair out, which Mike had just vacated, and sat down. Smiling, he said, "Okay, Mike, let's have it."

Mike took the opposite chair, and Judith slid into the empty chair facing Jac. Mike smiled to himself as he started to relate what he had heard from Maggie. "Maggie stated that the phone call Judith overheard most likely was directly from the governor's office." Jac gave a low whistle, and the look on Judith's face as it fell from a smile to a frown is all the ammunition Mike needed to continue. "It also was not one of the public lines into the governor's office but the private one that was used."

"Everyone knows that the Chesters have been trying to have children for years," stated Judith. "But do you think they would go the course of in vitro fertilization, and if yes, why here instead of Tallahassee General?"

"Tallahassee newspapers would have a field day with that news. I'm sure Calendar is one of the best in his field, and they would want the best. Plus, the doctor would probably keep that kind of news silent," said Jac. "He would also be covering his back by having the governor in his corner if something happens to his little side business."

"Judith, did you get the feeling that during the conversation, you heard that the client was going to call back?" asked Mike.

"I do not know about that. I only know that Frederick was very upset that there was a cancellation. I did not hear him making another appointment."

"So what do you propose, Jac?" said Mike.

"I think I'm going to finish that ride I never finished. Up to my uncle's home for lunch, and see what he thinks of this news. He is a close friend to James Chester, and I sure would like to talk to him about what we have found out about the doctor."

"Do not forget to mention that KaSandra had her baby and that it is going to be named after you," said Judith with a gleam in her eyes.

Mike's head swiveled around to face Judith so quickly that Jac thought it was going to fall off. "Where did you hear that, Judith? That the baby is going to be called Jac?"

"Are you trying to say something, Judith? And if so, spell it out," said Jac.

"Oh, no, not really. I just saw you upstairs with little Jac and got the feeling there is more going on in your head right now than you want anyone to know about. Am I right?"

Jac's smile widened, and he let out a little laugh. "I've always liked children, and little Jac Michael is not only a great-looking boy, but he is also named after Mike if you remember." With that, he got up from the chair and headed toward the door.

"Wait, what is going on here that I haven't heard all this? What is the baby's name anyway?" Both Judith and Jac shook their heads and said on the same time, "Jac Michael Cassillian." Then Judith added, "After you and Jac. Mike, we thought you knew."

"No, I didn't, and I think that's great," Mike said. "I've never had anyone named after me.

"Oh Jac," Mike calls after him, "why don't you take this drenched tape with you to your uncle's, and see if his people can save any of the information on it. Or I could take it to the police lab, but that might be risky right now, at least until we find out if Kaper is really alive or dead," said Mike.

Jac stopped in his tracks at the front door and came back. "Good thinking, Mike. I will get it out of the sink for it had been sitting in water ever since you yanked it out of the machine and dunked it to save as much as possible from disintegrating. I hope the water weakened the acid that burned it."

CHAPTER 27

It was a nice warm afternoon as Jac headed toward his uncle's home on the far end of the Keys, though he never saw the day for his mind was on the last time he had visited his uncle and what had occurred during that visit. He understood the reason for his uncle's motives regarding him for his lifestyle had been completely different from the accepted norm of the family. The head of the family always expected the males in the family to follow that practice. Jac had elected not to follow the norm of the business, but in all fairness, he had accepted all the fringe benefits that the males had indulged in for generations. This in itself would have been enough motive for his uncle to act the way he had, but then there was that promise he had made to his uncle to avoid jail time when he was sixteen. He had promised to sit and listen to all the reasons on why he should join the family business, even more so now that it was "respectable, upright, and accepted," which were a few of the adjectives his uncle had used that night. A promise was a promise, but who at sixteen would not have promised anything to get out of jail, especially when you hadn't done anything to get yourself into the situation? Well, almost nothing.

The family tradition was not for him. He wanted out, and on his own, he told his uncle. "So you are willing to accept all the comforts that have come your way since you were bailed out of jail and not accept any of the responsibility?" asked his uncle that night.

Most of that night, Jac had argued with his uncle that he had accepted the responsibility in a different way. He saw no reason to share in the dangers of going to jail or federal prison for some of the actions the other males in their family were taking.

Jac had remembered leaving his uncle early in the morning with everything still unresolved and gone to bed upstairs, but not to sleep. He had been in and out of horrid nightmares where he was either being chased by men with guns or on trial for his life. The judges gavel had been the last thing he remember as he waited to be sentenced and then awoke to the knocking at the door. *There must be a way to work for the family and stay out of the business*, he thought to himself as the bedroom door opened.

Jac didn't like the idea of going back to ask his uncle for a favor after that unresolved night, but Tony was the only one who could get through to the governor quickly and get him on their side in the upcoming sting. As Jac entered the gates of his uncle's estate, he wondered what kind of a mood he would find Tony in and if he should mention that Kass had her baby right away or wait for a more convenient time. After parking, he walked the short way to the front door and prepared himself for the upcoming overnight ordeal.

Spencer, Tony's live-in companion, answered the door and greeted him with a warm hello. "Mr. Jac, what a wonderful surprise to see you. Your uncle is in the conservatory and will be so pleased to know you're here. Should I announce you?"

"No, Spencer, I know the way and would rather surprise him myself," he stated.

"As you wish, Mr. Jac. Would you like something to drink or eat?"

"A nice stiff drink. No, better make it some tea, knowing uncle and the way he dislikes drinking before four o'clock."

"As you wish. Will that be Earl Grey sir?"

"Yes, that's great and something sweet if the cook has anything. Thanks, Spencer," Jac said as he walked the short distance to the conservatory—his uncle's favorite place in the whole estate. As he entered the warm room of the flower paradise, he caught the look of surprise on Tony's face.

"Jac, what brings you out here to see me?" he said without a trace of sarcasm for Jac rarely comes. *But he was quite warm*, Jac thought.

"Oh, some tea and conversation in this hothouse of yours."

"What? Nothing stronger?"

"Well, that sounds like the uncle I know, but after all, uncle, it's not even one thirty yet and a little early for me," Jac said with a smile on his face.

Since when? Tony thought but just smiled back and answered, "Well, good, shall I ring for Spencer?"

"No, he met me at the door, and I asked for it then. Hope you don't mind."

"Jac, why would I mind? You are my nephew. I love you. So come over here, and hold this stem for me while I tie it up for a sense of balance. Then we can sit down and have a breather."

"Tony," Jac began as he held the slender stem of a yellow rose whose fragrance reached up to meet his incoming inhale, which he found it quite pleasant, "when was the last time you talked with James Chester?"

It was Tony's turn to look questionably at his nephew and replied, "Well, it has been a good month for sure. I saw him at the last charity function for the new hospital wing. Why? What is going on in that head of yours now?"

"It seems that someone on his private line called our Dr. Calendar and cancelled an appointment last week. We, at the hotel, are under the opinion that someone might be looking for the doctor's services.

Tony put down the twine he had been holding, grabbed Jac's elbow, and turned him toward a small table set with the tea items Spencer had placed there. "I knew that the Chesters were having trouble having a baby for James confided in me. Are you thinking that Calendar might use his own sperm? And that's what you are concerned about?"

"Yes, for I'm sure that James has no idea what we know is going on at the clinic. What a perfect way to shield his alleged self-using sperm business than to have the governor of Florida in his front pocket if a baby is conceived."

"I see what you mean, but how did you get this information?"

"All I'll say is that it was a favor from a friend of a friend," Jac replied.

"Jac, I can't go to the governor and say that. He will think his private phone is tapped. That's against the law, and it could have been anyone in his office who used the phone."

"No, the number that was used was in his residence attached to the office and would most likely be used only by James or his wife. According to the females in my office," said Jac, "the Chesters have been trying to conceive for years and may be going in for the insemination route as a last resort. I'm not asking you to pry into their personal business. Just somehow mention our suspicion to him about Calendar, and see if he bites," said Jac.

As Jac finished his last word, he lifted his teacup and sipped, watching his uncle over the lip of the cup for a reaction. He realized that Tony was mulling over what he had said and was trying to come up with a plausible solution to Jac's problem.

"Are you sure this informant is convinced that the call came from the governor's private phone?"

"Yes, Uncle. It was a person at the phone company who let us know the information. I'm just concerned that the governor will get snarled up in Calendar's scams and cause a lot of problems for him and the state when it comes out what Calendar had done to all those couples."

"Yes, yes, I know, my boy," Tony said as he reached for his portable phone to place the call. After the phone rang several times, the secretary answered.

"The governor's offices. This is Janet, how can I help you?"

"Hi, Janet, this is Anthony Castello. Is the governor in, please?"

"Oh, Mr. Castello, so nice to hear your voice. Yes, the governor is in but on his other line. May I take a message, or would you like to hold?"

"Janet, can you have James call me back? I just wanted to discuss something with him over supper here at my home in the Keys. I thought maybe he and Margaret could get away for a few days of peace and quiet this weekend?"

"What a nice idea. He has been working so hard lately that it would do him good to get away for the weekend, and what good timing for his schedule is free. I will ask him to return your call as soon as he is finished with his conference call."

"Fine, Janet. I'll be at home for the rest of the afternoon and early evening. I'll be going out around eight for several hours, so if he could call before or after, it would be great."

"Thank you, Mr. Castello. That will be very convenient I'm sure. I'll give your message to the governor when he is free. Thank you again for calling."

Jac had been listening and asked, "Where are you going at eight? I had thought I'd stay the evening."

"That's what I was hoping for Jac. The outing was for you and me to have dinner at Victors. I would also like you here if the Chesters can make it this weekend, if you can arrange it."

"I think that can be arranged if I can bring some guests back with me."

"What? My nephew going out with a woman?" said Tony.

"Yes, actually, I was thinking of two people who could use a change of pace."

"Oh, that's just fine, Jac, but I was hoping you were seeing someone."

"Uncle, these two people would be even better. I was going to bring Kass and her new son over for the weekend."

Tony was speechless and very surprised but finally managed to say, "What? The baby is here?"

"Yes, she had a boy this morning and is going to name him Jac Michael Cassillian."

"Well, that's just wonderful, and even though it's not four o'clock yet, I think this calls for a drink. Though Jac Michael Scarin would have been better as his name."

"Uncle, before I forget, do you think you could get some of your people to work on this cassette? It got dunked in water to prevent it from destroying itself. The information it has can probably save me a lot of trouble with the police. This is from Kaper."

Before Jac left to go see his uncle, he asked Mike when he was heading to New York. Jac knew that a visit to his uncle's would probably last a few days, and he was in need of the information on whether Kaper was really dead or just trying to frame Jac.

Mike said, "I planned tomorrow after I check out the delivery boy a little further and hopefully get other leads and then head north."

Mike called the number for Fast Deliver, which Crystal had given him, and talked to the delivery person again, who had brought Jac cassette. Tim Clark, the deliver boy was very helpful. He remembered picking up the shoe box at a small downtown hotel on the beach and had wondered why such a cool-looking, sharply dressed guy like that man was staying at such a run-down hotel. Mike had asked him the name of the hotel, and Tim had said the Sleepy Lagoon. After thanking Tim, Mike headed for the hotel, knowing beforehand that Kaper would not be there or had not even stayed there. Upon reaching the reception desk at the Sleeping Lagoon, Mike took out a twenty-dollar bill and the picture Jac had given him of Kaper, which was taken at his mother's funeral several months earlier. Mike talked with the clerk. He had been right; no one looking like the man in the picture had stayed there. But a bartender standing there, waiting for some cash for his register asked to see the picture. After studying the photo for a minute, he said, "Sure, this is the guy who arrived in the Hotel Hilton's rent-a-motorboat and stayed for about an hour at the bar, waiting for someone."

"Can you tell me anything else?" Mike asked.

"Not really. He sat at the far end of the bar, minding his own business. He did have a box with him that he kept on patting. Then he would smile to himself. But that's about all. He left shortly after giving the box to a delivery kid, and I think he motored back to the other side."

Mike drove to the Hilton next and checked with the front desk clerk to see if any person matching Kaper's description had rented in the last few days. Neither the morning or evening front desk clerk recognized Kaper from his picture nor did the description Mike gave them, including the scar down his face. This did not surprise him. Kaper would not be stupid to stay even one night, but he checked with the rental booth on the beach and found, after showing his picture around, that Kaper had used the pool a couple of hours and rented the boat at 11:00 a.m. the past Tuesday. Mike figured that if Kaper had stayed in the area, he was now long gone, probably to one of the other Keys.

Mike did think that Kaper was alive and somewhere in the Keys. Kaper's nature would not let him leave town without knowing that Jac was in jail or about to be jailed for his death. Jac had received the tape of Kaper's death on Monday, and if the attendant at the bar was right, Kaper was alive on Tuesday.

CHAPTER 28

Receiving limited results in the Keys, Mike flew to New York to get as much information on the Senior Kalabrese's death. He first checked the main library in the circulation section for any articles related to what happened to Kalabrese and what was considered the truth. The lead article in the New York Times stated that the police found the multi-millionaire Theodore Kalabrese's dead body in his Manhattan penthouse late Saturday night at around ten o'clock after a mysterious caller, who had heard screams coming from the exercise room, called the police. On entering the area, the article reported the police found a body lying face down, and after further investigation, the body was identified as Theodore Kalabrese. Mr. Kalabrese Sr., seventy-six years old, was pronounced dead of an unknown origin. The body's face showed pure terror like he knew that he was about to die. Other than a large red mark on his forehead, there was not a scratch on the body.

The article went on to state that the police found, on searching the rest of the penthouse, that a portrait of Mr. Kalabrese, which was painted about four years previous by a well-known New York artist, had received a slash down the right side of the portrait's face. On seeing this, the police put out an arrest warrant for Kaper Kalabrese for questioning but later halted after the police were informed that the younger Kalabrese was resting in the local hospital after an assault on which he received twenty stitches to the face.

Finishing the article, Mike made a copy and left the library. His next stop was going to be the morgue and a talk with the police pathologist to see if there was anything found unusual on or in the body.

After Mike's review of Mr. Kalabrese's file, which was still in the unsolved files of the police homicide department, he visited Dr. Thomas Roman, a county coroner down in the police lab.

"Dr. Roman, thanks for meeting with me. I'm a detective, working on the Kalabrese case. I got from the newspaper report that he had a contusion on his head from a barbell. The police report believes he got the mark when he fell. But what about these other marks in the report?" asked Mike, "the ones the newspaper didn't report on, the ones on his upper arms?"

"Yes, on each upper arm, there were small cuts. Several going up and down and a large one that went sideways across the deltoid muscle," said Dr. Roman.

"Dr. Roman, were they made possibly by a device that was holding him so he could not move out of the way of a weapon? And if so, could he have died of a heart attack, maybe out of fear?"

"The autopsy showed that the heart muscle was not overly affected, but there were signs of high epinephrine adrenaline, which can put stress on the heart. Mr. Kalabrese did suffer a heart failure within the last two to three years. But from the police photos, now that you say it, those marks could have been made by some kind of a device that was holding him against something. But there were no marks on his back, so he couldn't have been pushed against the wall."

"It might have been the floor, if someone had put padding between him and the surface," exclaimed Mike. "How did his vertebrates look? Were any damaged?"

"Yes, I do believe that I wrote down somewhere…" His voice trailed off as he looked through his autopsy papers. "Yes, here, I wrote down that vertebrates 6, 7, and 8 were cracked, but that could have happen at any time with his age and a slight nudge."

"Would it be possible to have happen the night of his death, doctor?" Mike asked as he felt his own heart quicken.

"Yes, I would have to state that it could have happened during that time if he was pinned and could not move freely and was afraid of something, so he struggled to get free."

"Thank you, Dr. Roman. You have been most helpful."

CHAPTER 29

Jac sat in his office, staring out of the window at the ocean. He loved to watch the waves hitting the shore, but this time, his mind was going over the scenes from the last few nights. It started with Kass and Jac Michael rocking peacefully by the fire. JM's big blue eyes stared up at his mother as he sucked his third or fourth meal of the day.

Jac love watching the two of them together; JM's little round head nestled closed to Kass's breast, and those cherry-red lips sucked so greedily. Every so often, a drop or two would escape his lips and run oh so slowly down a chubby cheek. Kass would catch the milk with her finger and proceed to lick it while smiling down at him. She would softly continue to hum the song she heard from the piano down in the lounge, which was being played my Jac's uncle, Tony.

When Jac had returned to the hotel, he remembered and smiled at Kass's surprise, then he told her that she was to be pampered even more at his uncle's home for the weekend. He stretched the truth by saying that after he mentioned that she had the baby and that he was named after himself, Tony insisted that the two of them come for a weekend visit. Not speaking out loud his thoughts that he did not want to be alone in the house without protection from who knows what his uncle might think up for him next, he gathered up Kass and the baby and left for Half Moon, his uncle's estate.

Kass had lost some of her baby weight, and in doing so, she could probably fit back into her yellow sun outfit and the pink-and-gold long dress to wear for dinner Saturday night. *Probably lost it too fast*, she thought, and she would most likely hear about it when she went to her checkup on Monday. Jac had mention that Tony had invited the governor and his wife for the weekend, also most likely to warn them about Dr. Calendar.

Kass had always felt so warm toward Tony Castello ever since the moment she met him at the clinic of Dr. Calendar. He was even better than she remembered as he greeted her, JM, and Jac at the front door. He immediately took JM from her arms and walked out to the patio with him.

"Well, I hope you see him in time for his next feeding," said Jac with a laugh.

Spencer leaned over to take the bags that Kass had brought, and Jac said, "Oh, I can see that you must be so busy getting things organized for this weekend, with the governor and all coming. Where do you want Kass and the baby?"

"Mr. Tony has placed Ms. KaSandra and the baby in the front room, overlooking the ocean, but it is not necessary for you to help, Mr. Jac. Mr. Tony has extra people hired to do the cooking, serving, and such for these occasions. You will have the room next to Ms. KaSandra. Your own room, of course."

"Thank you, Spencer. Now, maybe we better join my uncle on the patio, or who knows what shape he will be in with that bundle he escaped with," said Jac.

Jac was smiling to himself over the memories when the phone rang, and Crystal told him that KaSandra had called and would be back at the hotel for lunch and wanted to speak with him.

"Thanks, Crystal. I'll be here. I'll just go and see what Joe has on the menu for the two of us. "Now what's on that smart mind of hers I wonder." he said to himself.

After making the phone call to the hotel, Kass said good-bye to Dr. Sharon and headed for her car. She sat in the car for a while and thought again about the wonderful weekend she just had and how much fun it was to be included in such interesting conversation and guests. The Chesters, James and Margaret, were just delightful people, and Margaret was so entranced with JM that it was too bad they had to hear about Dr. Calendar and his fraudulent schemes. "I must remember to ask Jac the news he heard from the Chesters about their dealing with Dr. Calendar," Kass said out loud as she started her car and headed to her rendezvous with Jac.

Kass was so late getting back that Jac had finished his lunch and gone out for a run. After hearing this from Crystal, Kass decided to get a chocolate shake from the kitchen and some rest before JM woke up from his nap, knowing Jac would be a good hour with his run.

Jac returned feeling refresh and in need of a shower. "Crystal, is Kass back yet?"

"Yes, she came in about five minutes after you left for your run and said she was going to relax for a bit before JM wanted his feeding."

"Thanks, if you need me, I'll be in my room for a while and then with Kass and the baby," said Jac as he headed up the stairs two at a time.

Jac, refreshed and wearing a clean change of clothes, stood holding JM on the patio of Kass's room. He was glad he had insisted that she change rooms after the baby came. She really needed the space, and he knew that she loved to sit out here in the early morning and feed JM while watching the new day arrive.

"Jac," Kass said from the door where she had been watching him, "do you think we could have dinner together later?" Jac heard her speaking but didn't register the words she was articulating.

He answered with a falter in his voice, "Did you ask me to dinner with you?" He raised his head from the baby and transferred his smile to her, and she nodded her head in reply.

"How much later are you talking about, Kass?" Kass eyes began to twinkle as Jac got up and walked across to where she stood. "It's 3:05 right now. Do you think you could be ready for a 7:30 reservation?" asked Jac. As he said this, he stroked the baby's head. His long fingers moved oh so gently across the small surface, letting the black wisps of hair filter through his fingers. Kass saw a slow smile widen Jac's lips and as he gazed down at the small boy. He asked again, "Will that give you enough time? I know the maitre d' and can always get the table next to the ocean."

"Seven thirty should be just fine, and I've heard they have the best steak in the Keys. Is that right?" said Kass.

"That right. Pick you up at 7:30, and wear something flowing. Oh, what about JM?"

"Crystal has been begging me to let her sit with him so that's covered."

Jac smiled at Kass and left to make the arrangements. *She wants steak and maybe some of that Ma Donna White wine she likes. If I didn't know better I'd think she planned that whole scene.*

Planned it was an understatement for KaSandra had decided to get Jac more involved in her and JM's life. *I know he loves the baby. By the way he is always holding and hanging around him, he would probably be willing to adopt him. After the sting is over, I'll give more thought to that subject, but what do I wear tonight?*

Seven twenty-five. One more look in the mirror and off I go to meet the man I've been in loved with since I was in school with him.

Smiling at her reflection, Kass thought, *Yes, that exercise group I joined two months ago has really helped me get my figure back.*

KaSandra had chosen a lemon yellow sheath dress with a neckline that revealed her rounded breasts. The skirt fell to the floor but was loose enough for her still-slightly round center. The earrings were a yellow shade, which enhanced her golden-brown hair, and a single gold chain held the two-karat diamond that laid at the base of her neck. The necklace was a gift from Jac after JM was born.

Jac left his office just as Kass was leaving JM's room after checking on him and Crystal. He had changed into a tan pair of slacks, white linen shirt with short sleeves, with a tan collar to match his slacks. The shirt was opened slightly to reveal his darkened skin and a gold St. Christopher medal nestling in his black hair. His barrel chest and broad shoulders filled the shirt that ended at his waist, revealing a slightly band of fat, which was the area Kass delighted in grabbing. Kass spied Jac just as he looked up to see her coming out of the baby's room. She had pressed the button for down, and after seeing Jac, she decided to take the stairs to show off what she was wearing as she descended. Jac was watching her closely as she took one step after another. *That skirt caps her fanny nicely*, he thought. *She always had a nice figure but only better now that she had JM, more round and not so thin.* Kass reached the bottom step, and Jac took her hand and kissed it. He noticed the slightly revealing curve to her breasts at the same time, and it made his pulse quicken.

"How nice you look, Kass. That yellow really suits you," he said, handing her a white rose.

"Thank you," she purred and lifted the rose to her nose for the scent. Jac shifted her hand to his arm, still covering it as he turned her toward the restaurant.

Ten o'clock. Kass let out a contented sigh as she walked along the beach with Jac. "Is everything all right?" he asked.

"Everything is just fine, Jac, but I do have a question."

"Yes?"

"How is the sting going against Dr. Calendar? Don't you think that if he gets cornered, he might cause trouble for JM and me?"

"Trouble? How, Kass?" Jac asked.

"Well, think about it, Jac. JM is his kid and mine, and all he has to do is claim him. He might even try to take him away, stating I had consented to sex with him. It would be my word against his for no one saw a thing that he did, not even me."

Jac stopped walking and faced Kass, placing his hands on her shoulders. "Kass, stop worrying," he said.

"I doubt if he will start anything for that would make it worse for him, and I'm sure he would not want his dealings publicized any more than they will be."

"Then how is Tony coming with the involved couples? Are they going to bring charges? I can now understand why they didn't want to rock the boat. I don't know what I'd do if something happened to JM." Jac put a protective arm around Kass to help soothe her fears, and they continued to walk down the beach toward the hotel.

"Kass, I know that we've known each other since we were kids, and we get along so well. I love the baby..." his voice trailed off as he stopped and looked out at the ocean, wondering if this was the right time to ask Kass to marry him. Turning back, he kissed her lips; first slowly, gently, and when she responded to him, more boldly. Both wanted to be in each other's arms and wanted to be kissing each other, hoping the other would feel the same way.

"Jac, I think I know what you are trying to say, but let's just wait a little longer until this mess is taken cared of and Dr. Calendar is put away. Then baby and I will be out of danger. Is that okay?" Kass was looking into Jac's eyes and saw something she had hope for but was too afraid to speak out loud, especially to him. Finding her voice, she asked, "Jac, are you all right?"

Instead of answering, Jac bent down and scooped her into his arms and walked to the hotel service elevator just off the beach entrance. As the door closed on the floor, he lifted his head from Kass's lips just long enough to enter his quarters. He placed her on the sofa, telling her to stay put and left the suite for Kass's room. Scooping up the baby and helping Crystal in the taxi for her apartment, he returned to his suite, placing JM into a bassinet.

Kass left Jac's suite for hers when she saw him helping Crystal on with her sweater and leading the way to the taxi. Reaching her room, she pulled open her closet and removed a pink lingerie set with slippers and hurriedly changed, then ran back to Jac's room so she would not be missed. Upon hearing Jac's return with the baby and going into his nursery, she slipped in and returned to the divan where he had left her.

Jac laid JM on his back and stood looking at him sleeping so peacefully. His eyelashes lay across his cheeks, and those rosy little lips made movements like he was sucking milk from his mother's breast. His thin long fingers opened and closed as if reaching for something in his sleep. *What a wonderful boy you are*, he thought, *and soon I'm going to make you my son.* Covering the boy with a blanket, he left the room to return to Kass in the living room. He found her stretched out with her right arm under her head, sound asleep. Bending down, he kissed her beautiful lips and whispered, "Kass. Kass."

Kass laid there inhaling his shaving lotion and receiving his kisses when he suddenly licked her cheek and made her laugh. Opening her eyes, she found she was almost nose to nose with a great smile covering his face.

"Are you anticipating something here?" he asked.

"I don't know what you mean," she said shyly.

"Oh really? Then what is all this?" His arm made a sweeping movement down her body, and his eyes followed.

"Oh, I just changed into something more relaxing." She slipped from under his arm, off the divan, and walked over to the doors that looked out on to the patio. She opened the doors just as there was a knock at the door. Jac went to open it, not taking his eyes off Kass's lingerie, which showed off a wonderful body underneath. Standing back, he allowed a smiling Joe holding a huge tray full with food to enter.

Behind him, Peter pushed a cart full of crystals, flowers, wine, a coffee urn, and desserts all to set up a beautiful table on the patio.

Spying KaSandra, who was standing now on the patio, he walked to her and whispered that maybe she should go inside until Peter got things set up. Kass smiled at the admiring looks her evening attire received as she glided into the living room chair and out of their way. Jac also caught the looks she was receiving and felt a little irritation for his employees. He wanted Kass to himself even though he knew the men meant nothing by their glances. Who wouldn't look at a beautiful woman? As Jac struggled with this new emotion, he didn't see the smile on Kass's face as she watched him. She asked, "When did you do all this?"

Jac's face returned the smile, and he said, "Well, it took a little doing considering the hour, but the thought of overtime must have been a good incentive." Jac and Kass vaguely saw the two men finish and disappear, leaving the two of them standing together. Jac reached for her hand and softly pulled her out into the warm breezy air under the moonlight and they walked to the table set for romance.

Joe and Peter had outdone themselves for the table had a beautiful bouquet of flowers made up of mixed daisies, red rose and carnations, and baby's breath. Crystal plates, glasses, and platters, with fresh fruit, crackers and cheese in different shapes excited the eyes, and on the side table was a bottle of Rothschild Cognac, which was their favorite.

"Kass, may I pour you a glass?"

"Yes, but first, let's take this tie and jacket off and maybe those shoes. You are in your own suite now. Remember?"

"When you look like that, I'm not sure I remember anything." He pulled her to him and kissed her lightly at first, and then with more emotion, he bend down once more and lifted her into his arms, heading for the bedroom.

"Stop," she said. Giving Jac a start, Kass pointed to the cognac, and Jac tipped her slightly toward the bottle and glasses, and she grabbed them as they proceeded to the bedroom. Placing her on the bed, he removed his clothes under the watchful eyes of his companion. Smiling, he crawled into bed. Kass handed him his glass, and they clinked.

"To our future," they both said. Kass felt the warmth of the liquid and the tingle of Jac's hands as he ran it down her back, first taking the right and then the left lingerie strap with it.

Kass woke feeling happy and refreshed, and looking up, she saw the smiling face of Jac, who was holding the baby in his arms while the baby cooed back at him. "Jac, what time is it?"

"About feeding time for this little guy, and I think around two o'clock." She sat up, took JM, and offered him her breast. He sucked greedily at first, and as his stomach got full and warm, he sucked slower until he fell asleep. Kass placed him gently in his bed and joined Jac on the patio for coffee and fruit. The moon glistened off the ocean, and it was still warm as she sunk into her chair next to the man she now knows loved her deeply.

CHAPTER 30

After Mike left the morgue, he went to see Mr. Kalabrese's old valet, who was now retired and living with his daughter. The address in the police report stated that a Mr. Edward Towers lived at 740 Monte Calm Place, some exclusive condominium on upper Fifty-ninth Street in Manhattan. Mike first called Mr. Towers and asked if it would be convenient for them to talk about Mr. Kalabrese's death. Mike explained that he was working for Mr. Jac Scarin and that Jac was concerned about some mysterious unanswered questions. Edward Towers told Mike,

"Come on along, but I'm sure I cannot add anything more than what I told the police already."

At about four o'clock, Mike was sitting in a spacious living room overlooking the Manhattan River with a very starched-looking older man who was about seventy-five years old and still had a very firm handshake.

"Mr. O'Hara, it is nice to meet you. How is Mr. Jac?" said Edward Towers.

"He is fine but a little concerned over Mr. Kalabrese's death for Kaper has been suggesting to Jac that it might have been something other than an accident."

"Oh, poor, Mr. Kaper. I did suggest that I'd stay on for a while until he decides what he wants to do with the penthouse and all, but he insisted that I had worked all those years for his father and him and it was time for me to relax and enjoy my retirement."

"When was the last time you saw Kaper, Mr. Towers?" Mike asked.

"Oh, three days ago…no, four. He stopped up here and gave me that statue of The Thinker over there. I had always admired it ever since he gave it to his father before he was…imprisoned. I never really understood why Mr. Senior Kalabrese did not square it for Kaper with the IRS and keet him out of jail. Bad blood there…" And his voice trailed off.

"Mr. Tower, about the night that Kalabrese died, do you know who called the police?"

"No. You see, I was out for the evening, visiting my daughter and her family. She has three boys, or rather, we have them now. But that's neither here nor there. You were asking about that night? I came in at about 10:30 and found all the police here. The only thing mysterious about that call, Mike…May I call you Mike?" Mike nodded, and Edward continued. "Is that a phone call was made on the study phone at 10:17 that evening, and who made it is the question."

"Mr. Towers."

"Oh, call me Edward, please."

"Edward, how do you know that a phone call went out at that time?"

"You see, I paid all the bills for Mr. Kalabrese for years and did so right up until a month ago. He never trusted anyone else to do it. And then Mr. Kaper told me that he was having the attorneys do it now. I thought it odd that Mr. Kalabrese, Kaper, used the one in the office when there is an extension in the exercise room, but then maybe he needed some paperwork or something. I don't know."

"Did you ever tell this to the police?" Mike questioned.

"No, for you see, I didn't pay the bill until at least a month after his death."

"Tell me, Edward, do you know if Mr. Kaper is going to keep the penthouse or not?"

"No, absolutely not. Kaper told me it had too many bad memories. I believe he's got it on the market right now, selling everything, furniture and all."

"Oh, so Kaper is not living there now?" asked Mike.

"No, why do you ask?" Edward replied.

"Oh, I just thought I would like to look over the exercise room and see if I could get a feel as to what happened there."

"That's no problem. Mr. Kaper left me a key. You see, the swimming pool in this building is used by the older people so much that the kids hate to go down there. They are always scolded for making too much noise. So Mr. Kaper said that until the place is sold, the boys could use the pool there at his place. We can go over there right now if you like."

"Yes, Edward, if it's not too much trouble."

"Not at all. I'll tell the boys. They would probably love to go for a swim."

Edward, his three grandsons, and Mike entered the penthouse of the late Theodore Kalabrese, and Edward showed Mike to the exercise room before following his three boys down to the building pool. As Mike looked around the fairly big room, he saw where the body was found by the marking on the floor. Kaper had not even cleaned the room up. He really must have hated this place. Or maybe he left it for the realtors. There doesn't seem to have been anyone interested in seeing the penthouse of millionaire Senior Kalabrese. Thank goodness it has remained a crime scene. If it had been cleaned up, there would be no reason to look for all the evidence would be washed away.

Mike started walking the grid from one corner to the next, looking for anything that might have been overlooked. After an hour of crisscrossing the floor, Mike was about ready to give up when he spotted something caught in the binding of the workout mat. Mike's adrenaline seemed to move a little faster as he reached in to his briefcase to retrieved a tweezer, and very gently, he pulled from the mat what seem to be a small piece of skin.

He wondered how it got there. It looked like lizard's skin in its skeleton form. Mike smoothly placed the material into a plastic evidence bag, then into his case. As he turn to leave the room, Edward and the boys showed up at the door.

"Did your search prove helpful, Mike?" asked Edward.

"Well, it wasn't a total waste of time. I can see your quandary over the business phone because this one works just fine in here," said Mike, pointing to the extension.

CHAPTER 31

As the sun hit Jac's face, he stretched and rolled over, expecting to see a beautiful face next to him. The bed was empty, and there was no sound in the suite. Rising, he strolled into the living room, calling Kass's name. She was gone and so was the baby. Half an hour later, Jac found Kass on a beach chair under an umbrella, holding a sleeping JM and quite drowsy herself. As he sat down on the sand, she stirred, smiled at him, and said, "Good morning."

"What are you doing down here?" he asked.

"Oh, JM was starting to get fussy, and the beach looked like a wonderful place to calm him down, so I came out." Her voice stopped as she saw his face. "I'm sorry, Jac, but you looked so peaceful that I didn't have the heart to wake you. We can still have breakfast together."

Jac smiled and said, "Well, if that's the best you can offer, I'll accept." Helping her to her feet and taking the baby from her arms, they both strolled up to the restaurant.

An hour later, they were still sitting over coffee, looking at the beach with dirty dishes in front of them when Mike grabbed a chair and said, "Hey, it's my turn to hold him," as he reached for JM. Kass laughed as she saw the look on Jac's face when Mike lifted the baby from him and sat down again.

"Mike, you are in a good mood. When did you get back from New York?"

"About two hours ago," Mike said to all listening to him but smiled down at the boy in his arms. JM was smiling up at him and cooing to Mike's gentle pats on his back. Looking up, Mike said, "Got quite a lot accomplished and found out some very interesting information."

"Yes?" said KaSandra as she waited for Mike to continue. Mike was so enthralled with the small bundle in his arms that he almost did not feel Kass's kick on his shoe. "Mike."

Mike looked up and smiled. "Just a minute, KaSandra. I almost have him asleep." Putting the baby down in his pushchair, Mike straightened up and said, "That is some kid."

"Thank you," said Kass, "but what about your news?"

"You see," said Mike, pouring himself a cup of coffee and sitting down again, "after I looked over the pictures taken at the scene of Theodore Kalabrese's death, which was stored at the police morgue, and after I talked to the county coroner, Dr. Roman, who explained his thoughts on how the marks on the upper part of the corpse's arms got there, I went to see a Mr. Edward Towers, his—"

"Stop, stop, Mike. Back up a little bit to the marks on the arms," said Kass and Jac together.

Mike laughed and said, "Maybe. All right, let me start at the beginning. When I got into New York, I went straight to the public library and looked up the newspaper account for Senior Kalabrese's death. It gave all the details of the supposed heart attack and that an autopsy was scheduled at the police forensic department. So I made a copy of the article and decided to go to the police morgue and talk to the attending coroner or police forensic specialist. After seeing those photos taken at the scene, I had a lot of questions. For you see, there were purple scratches and contusions on the upper arm like Kalabrese was being held by something, or something was strapped around his upper arms. Then I went and saw Mr. Edward Towers, who was Senior Kalabrese's valet, and asked him what was going on with the penthouse and if Kaper was going to live there. Edward was quite informative. He said the place was on the market for Kaper did not want to stay there with all the memories. Also, he said that the office phone was used, and he wondered why for there was one in the exercise room. Later, we went over to the penthouse, and I had a look at the mat where the body was found. Nothing really showed up there, and I was about to leave when I spied something strange for an exercise room. Caught in the bindings of the floor mat was a piece of lizard skin. I've taken it over to a lab I use here, and they are testing it for what kind of lizard."

"Why do you think it is a lizard? It could be the shredded skin of a snake that is molding," asked Jac.

"Well, sure, but what would a snake be doing in the exercise room of that penthouse?" said Mike.

"It's a horrid thought," continued Jac, "but Kaper was always having snakes around when he was younger, and his father make him keep them in his part of the building. Theodore was deathly afraid of them, and Kaper knew that."

"That puts a different spin on the death. The coroner found high levels of adrenaline in Senior's body at the examination, and if Kaper had somehow frightened his father enough with a snake, that could have caused another heart attack," said Mike.

"So you're saying," said KaSandra, "that Kaper bound his father to that mat so he couldn't get away and then brought in his pet snake and caused his father's death by pure fright? That's murder."

"That's a possibility. Exercise can raise your adrenaline too, so the doctors presumed that was the cause of death, not fright," said Mike.

"The question now is how do we prove it to the police and get Kaper for his father's death, supposing that Kaper is still alive," said Jac.

"Oh, he's still alive. Believe me," said Mike.

CHAPTER 32

A Jade Green Jaguar was just passing number 2004 on Big Torch Key and was heading further down the highway with a fair blond-haired driver. The man in real expensive clothes was thoroughly enjoying the sun and the wonderful weather that the Keys always seem to have. That driver was Kaper Kalabrese, and his mission in the Keys was to hide out long enough for a Jac Scarin to be charged with his death.

Jaguars were seldom seen in such good condition down in the general area unless the owner had money, and Tony Castello know all the wealthy owners and what they drove. This one was new, and the driver caught Tony's attention for he looked rather familiar. Tony was driving out of his driveway at 2004 Big Torch Key and was on his way to a meeting with the governor. Still pondering the stranger in the Jaguar as Tony drove back to his estate three hours later, he suddenly realized who the driver might be, Kaper Kalabrese.

Upon reaching his study, Tony picked up the phone and called Jac to relate what the governor had said about Dr. Calendar.

"Jac, Tony here, do you have a few minutes to talk?" Jac was still sitting at the table in the restaurant with the others and said, "Sure. Is this about Calendar?"

"Yes, I've talked to the governor, and he said—"

"Wait, Tony. Let us go into my office for I'm sitting with Kass, Judith, and Mike, and I want them to hear if it's all right with you."

"Sure, I'll hold."

There was a pause, then Jac said, "Okay, Tony, you are on the speaker phone. Go ahead."

"The governor confirmed that he and his wife, Margaret, were seeing Dr. Calendar for fertility problems, and his wife had a treatment about six months ago that was unsuccessful. They had made another appointment but had to cancel for Margaret wasn't feeling well."

"So that was the phone call I overheard when Calendar got so angry. Thank goodness they didn't go back," said Judith.

"Yes, Judith, and that's what I told the governor when he asked why I was inquiring about Dr. Calendar and their dealings with him."

"Tony, Mike here. Did you happen to inform the governor about our suspicions and all the other couples that might be implicated in this mess?"

"Yes, Mike, I did. Chester was not pleased for he had specifically picked the doctor for privacy and his exceptional skills. Finding out this information at this time of reelection, especially if it leaks out to the press, could be dire to his career. The governor also asked how we were planning to catch Dr. Calendar, and I filled him in on our plans. James also volunteered to help us with a sample of Dr. Calendar's DNA, and I didn't ask how," said Tony.

"At least, Uncle, that saves you the trouble of calling some favors of your own," said Jac.

"Why, Jac, I don't know what you are talking about. Business is just business," said Tony. "Oh, by the way, I have the cassette back from my experts, and you will be surprised at how much they were able to save. Nasty business what Kaper is up to. While I'm speaking of Kaper, I think I saw him driving up the Big Torch Key Drive this morning. If it wasn't him, it was his double even though I haven't seen the guy in years, but he's kind of hard to miss him with that pale blond hair. Always made me think he was sick with his hair so white since when he was a kid. Well,

I guess I'll be seeing all of you on Friday when all the couples involved are gathering here for an update this weekend. James and Margaret thought they might join us to hear what these couples have to say. Say, Jac, why don't you all come up early in the day and get some sun and such by the pool?"

"Thanks, that sounds like a wonderful idea, if lunch is thrown in." Jac grinned as he replied.

Everyone heard Tony laughing over the phone, then he said, "Thats my boy. Always looking for something to fill his stomach. Tell you what, Jac, I'll even throw in dinner if you and I can have a little talk."

Jac picked up the phone and said, "Sure, Uncle. Why not?" Then after a minute or so of listening, he hung up the phone.

Turning to the rest of the group in the room, Jac said, "Well, that's good news about the governor, especially that he wants to help. Mike, do you have anyone on that side of the Keys who can do a little searching around and see if they can locate Kaper on the quiet?"

"Sure, I'll get right on it." Mike got up and left the room with Judith right on his heels.

Kass look up at Jac and asked, "Are you all right?"

"Oh sure." He let out a deep sigh. "It's just my uncle and his constant approach of trying to get me back into the family business."

"Is that so bad?" asked Kass in a whisper. "Hasn't all the families gone legal now?"

"Well, yes and no. The old men are still doing a lot of stuff the old way and not get caught, while the younger generation are getting caught when they are stupid enough not to listen."

"Tony doesn't want you in the business for that kind of stuff, does he?" asked Kass.

"No, he wants me to go back to using my law degree to protect the rights of the family's hot shots."

"Did he tell you that?"

"No, he didn't come right out and say it that way, but the whole crux of the problem between him and me is that I've benefited from the family's payoffs without doing my fair share to help according to Tony."

"Is he right?"

"Kass, I haven't taken anything from the family since I was a teenager, and we got into that trouble with the car," Jac said.

"Oh, don't remind me. I still don't know how you talked me into it," said Kass.

"Come on now, you loved that wild ride. Carl and I got you and Pat out of the way before the cops came anyway." Jac sighed again. "Granted, Tony kept our record clean, and we stayed out of jail, but what he wants now in return is keeping seasoned criminals out of jail that should be there, even if they are family. That's why I ended up in the hospital two years ago and almost lost my life. No, I'm out, and I'm staying out." Kass stepped forward and put her arms around him for a hug just as the door opened and in walked Judith.

CHAPTER 33

Frederick was dressing with utmost care for today was Wednesday, and a very beautiful lady was coming to see him. What he had planned would not only put more of his genes into this world through an offspring, but that wonderful-looking ebony skin and body will be within his grasp for at least an hour, and he was going to savor it to his heart's content.

Yes, his thoughts continued. "I will tell (Ms. Judith that I should extract her eggs now since she is ovulating for according to her information, this should be the time. I'll give her the local anesthetic for the discomfort, and it will make her drowsy but still awake. Then I can have her at the same time and have both my sperm inside of her and her eggs for a later date. What a wonderful afternoon I have prepared for myself," he said as he smiled at his image in the mirror.

On the other side of the Keys, Mike O'Hara was sitting once again with Judith, Kass, and Jac as they discussed the upcoming visit to the Calendar Clinic. Mike was sure that the doctor was going to try something, and unless Judith was not wired, she would be his next victim. "Judith, if I read this man right, he is going to want to do it today, and I have just the right thing here to track you with and hear your every word," said Mike.

"Why are we moving everything up? I thought we were going to have someone out in the waiting room ready to jump in if I said the word?" asked Judith.

"Judith that was and is the plan, but from what the couples said last night at Tony's, Mike is right. There is a very good possibility that Calendar is over-eager and might try today, and can you really refuse? Remember, all he is going to say to you is that he wants to extract your eggs, not go through the operation of implanting the egg with sperm today. Most of the women last night believe that he did the implanting of his sperm at the time of egg retrieval," said Jac.

"So who is going to be out there with me?" asked Judith, her voice showing a little strain.

"Mike knows this policewoman in Miami who's done undercover work, and he's requested that she come down here to help us out. The governor himself called her department chief to verify it. They are saying she is your best friend who's flown in just to be at your side."

"Oh." Everyone heard a great sigh come from her lips. "So where am I suppose to wear my bug this time? In the retrieval room, you do not have a lot of clothes on. I will probably have a hospital gown," said Judith.

Mike reached across the table with his fist closed and offered Judith something in his hand. She put her hand out and received a tiny stud diamond earring. "Oh, it is beautiful and looks so real," Judith said as Mike left the room.

"It is real and also is your wire, compliments of the Miami Police Department, who let us borrow them." Judith looked around the room for Mike and could not see him but could hear him just as when he was sitting next to her.

"Where are you?" asked Judith.

"I'm out here, standing next to Crystal," came Mike's reply. "Say, hi sweetie. To those at the table in the bar." She heard Crystal's pretty little laugh and then heard her say, "Hi, everyone. Wow, this is amazing." Then they heard the front door open and heard Mike say to someone, "Nice timing there, my pretty one. We were just testing the package your boss sent down via UPS yesterday."

There was the sound of a bag dropping, and then the most appealing southern drawl was heard over the studs that Judith held in her hand. "Hi to you too." Princess was a woman about five foot six, between thirty to thirty-five years, and with a form that showed a well-rounded workout routine. She gave off the idea that she could handle herself in every situation that came her way. Her rich deep-spoken voice was not from Florida but perhaps Tennessee or Alabama. As she spoke, she drawled out her voice in a strong commanding flow. "Oh, don't let me bother you, sweetie, for I've known these two for years, ever since Mike here was on the force and Jac would come in and get him to do some of the strangest investigation work for him."

"Mike," said a coy voice, then came a long silence, and Crystal cleared her throat in embarrassment. Then from the bar area, Mike and the mysterious voice heard the laughter of Jac coming from the studs in Crystal's hand.

"Mike, are you ever going to change? You know, you two, we can hear everything. That was some kiss."

Before Jac even got the words out of his mouth, Mike was walking back into the bar with a small and very pretty black woman on his arm. who wore a great big smile.

"Everyone, I would like you to meet Princess Henderson of the Miami undercover unit. Princess, this is Kass, Judith, and of course, you know him," Mike said, pointing to Jac.

With a firm hand shake, Princess greeted the women and was about to give Jac a kiss when she change her mind and hugged him instead. "What no kiss for me….?" The *E* came out of his mouth slightly muffled for she was kissing him passionately on the lips. Now, it was Mike's turn to laugh.

"Well, what is this? Old home week? I sure hope you two are having fun at the expense of the women in the room." Kass's face took on a very surprised look for she was embarrassed that those words came off her lips, and she caught the most interesting expression on Jac's face. Mike was handing the other stud to Judith as Princess took his chair, which was next to Jac, and smiled at Kass.

"Excuse me for interrupting," said Judith, "but why the name?"

"Why? Don't you like it? Oh well, my late husband always called me that, and that's the only name he ever used for me. So everyone in our social group just picked it up, and after he died, I just kept answering to it. I guess that's why I have that name now. Does that answer your question, Juuuudith?

"Mike, if her mouth is any indication of her skill and ability as an undercover person, I guess I am in good hands," retorted Judith, completely ignoring Princess.

With that remark, Princess roared with a deep throaty laugh and slapped Judith on the arm. "Girl friend, you're all right, and if Princess bothers you, then call me Janet."

Judith smiled and whispered loud enough for everyone to hear, "I am not your girl friend. Where we are going into this lions den, Princess would be just perfect. You cannot be a mouse with the doctor."

"Okay. If you two are finished sizing each other up, maybe we should talk about our plans," said Mike. "I gather that everyone can see how strong and sophisticated this little earring is? Judith, most likely, even if you have to disrobe, you won't have to take off any jewelry."

"I never had to before, and anyway, he has seen me in studs the last time I was there. Remember, KaSandra? I borrowed yours," said Judith.

"Yes." Princess looked up in the direction of Kass's voice and saw her holding a baby with his blanket over her shoulder, covering the fact that he was feeding. "Excuse me for feeding JM like this, but I didn't want to miss anything."

"Oh, is that one of the babies in this case?" stated Princess as she got up and asked Kass if she could see him. Kass, who love to show JM off just uncovered the baby's head and smiled.

"He's beautiful, but I thought the doctor was fair with blue eyes, and this baby's complexion is dark. You're lucky, KaSandra. He is beautiful. Some of the babies I heard are an awful lot like the doc in complexion." Just then, JM stopped drinking and turned his head to the strange voice and smiled, and Princess saw his very blue eyes.

"Wow! The color of his eyes is just marvelous. May I hold him?" Kass nodded and lifted JM up for Princess to hold. Surprisingly, Princess's face and body language changed completely as she held the baby and cooed to him. Again, the looks of amazement went around the table, and finally, Judith said, "Look, I think we have better get back to business. We got work to do."

"Oh, sorry. Sure, that's right," said Princess, becoming all business as she handed Kass the boy and sat down again.

CHAPTER 34

The meeting ended with everyone knowing exactly how to proceed and what they each had to do. Their guest, Thomas Lesueur, who bombed Jac boathouse and was now working for Jac, would be instructed on his part. After the initial meeting that included Princess, Mike went to the hotel phone and told Thomas that his presence was needed. Tony had suggested a little accident to happen to the electrical system in the clinic of Dr. Calendar since that would be right up his alley. Thomas was to get into the office under the guise that he was an electrician and stall long enough to spoil the specimens by lowering the freezing thermostat. Also, he was to be a close-at-hand back up if anything went wrong in the operating room for he would be carrying a bug.

Thomas was so excited to be part of the sting and to be doing something legit that after the meeting, he blabbed all about the job he was working on to Mabel, his newest girl. Mabel said, "Oh, honey, that makes me so excited that you kind of make me want to do something to celebrate with you, if you catch my drift." Thomas caught her drift all right, and the two of them disappeared into his room.

The appointment time could not come fast enough for Judith for she just wanted to get into action. The waiting around made her tense, and she did not want to act any different around Dr. Frederick Calendar. Princess arrived at ten minutes to nine and looked smashing in a creamed-colored pantsuit with a light brown blouse and matching sandals and handbag. The cream with the brown drew out her lovely brown-toned skin. She wore her hair long in the back, and the rest twisted around her head and held there with silk scarf. "Good morning," she said as she placed herself in the seat opposite of Judith. "Do I have time for a little breakfast? I'm starved."

"Yes," said Judith, stifling a yawn and smiling back at her. "My appointment is not until 10:30, and he, the doctor, never seem to be on time."

"Are any of them ever? When I have to go in for a physical, I'm always waiting at least twenty minutes after my appointed time. I always give them thirty minutes after my given time, and then I'm out of there. The male doctors are worse than females. Say, you look nice. That peach color is so flattering on you."

Judith was wearing a sleeved straight cotton sundress in peach that ended above her knees, the diamond stud earrings, and a flower-shaped pin in silver. Finishing the outfit were peach-colored pumps with matching bag.

Judith sat there in silence, sipping her coffee and thinking that a year ago, she would not have been caught dead in such an outfit or going to a doctor to have her eggs removed for the purpose of starting a baby even though she thought it would be nice to have the eggs on ice for the future. How times have changed. Looking up at Princess, she suddenly realized that she had not received a bug to hear the magic words "finished yet."

"Where is your bug?" asked Judith.

Princess smiled and touched a small-sized gold butterfly that held her scarf in place. "I would not go on any assignment without my butterfly. Now remember, Judith, do not let him enter you for he will probably be fully excited and wanting to relieve himself. Did you take the pill that I gave you to prevent pregnancy this morning?" asked Princess.

"Yes, but do you really think it was necessary?" answered Judith. "After all, I am going to be awake. He will probably give me a local."

"Remember, the other women victims did not know when he impregnated them, and they thought they were also awake. He must have made up a combination of a local pain reliever and slipped in a mild sleeping agent just enough to make his subjects too drowsy to fight back or remember afterward. Remember, he has been doing this for years. Some of those couples up at Mr. Castillo's have children who are between five and ten years old. Oh, Judith, if you do find that, you can't get the code words 'finished yet' out for the effect is too strong on you. Just say my name or *help*. I will be listening and so will the other police officers who are waiting not too far away from the clinic, just out of sight, and will advance when they hear the password or call for help," said Princess.

Jac had listened to all the preparations and then announced that he was still working with his uncle on a lawsuit and was taking a backseat but would stay in constant contact with Mike, who was going to be with the police. Jac had stressed to Princess that she had to keep Judith safe. When Jac left to join his uncle, he kissed Judith on the cheek and wished her well.

"Wow," said Princess, "what up with him? I don't think I've ever seen him so serious."

The others at the table exchanged glances, and KaSandra said as casually as possible, "The case that he and his uncle are working on has something to do with the government, and Jac always get up tight with that kind of business."

"Yes, I've noticed he does get involved with some juicy cases over the past few years. Maybe later on, we should talk about me doing some work for him," said Princess.

"Oh no you don't, sweetheart. There is one PI working with him right now, and that's me."

"Well all right. It was just a thought," said Princess as she stretched and got to her feet. "Judith, it's show time."

CHAPTER 35

Jac drove out of his parking spot and headed for his uncle's for a meeting with a member of the family. He finally gave in to his uncle after many arguments about responsibility and keeping one's promises. "After all, Jac there is no one better than you to handle the family's' affairs," Tony had said. Jac promised to do his share of the business as long as it didn't go against his conscience and the law.

Even though he had promised himself that he was going to stay out of the family business, he was looking forward to getting back into a little litigation. He was certainly not going to tell his uncle Tony what he thought about having him under his thumb; *I would never have time for my own work.* He drove the Porsche up the long driveway and parked in the semicircle. Walking across to the house, he noticed a black limousine parked right in front of the door with the driver standing, waiting for his client inside.

Before reaching the door, it was opened not by Spencer but his uncle who reached out and took Jac by the elbow and directed him toward the large study off the entrance hall. This room was hardly ever used for it was too formal for his uncle's taste. Jac often wondered why he didn't redecorate it into a more casual manner like the rest of the house. Upon entering the study, Jac noticed a rather elegantly dressed woman standing at the terrace door, staring out. She turned to quickly as they entered, and she spilled what she was drinking.

"Oh dear," she said and started to fall, reaching for the chair. Jac moved faster than his uncle and reached the woman to stead her, gently helping her into the chair. His uncle started to introduce him to the woman whom Jac estimated to be between the age of seventy-five and eighty. She smiled up at Jac, and raising her hand, she said, "I know Anthony. This is Jac, and I would know him anywhere. He is as handsome as you and has his mother's eyes and smile. Jac, kneel down here so I can get a real good look at you."

Jac smiled down at the lady in front of him and knelt down as he was bidden, wondering who she was. This woman with the expressive and searching eyes looked so familiar to him. He was sure he had seen her before but as a much-younger woman.

"Dear boy, don't tell me you have forgotten who I am. After all those summers that you, your cousin, and all those friends like what was his name, the one with the pale, pale hair?"

"Kaper Kalabrese."

"Yes, yes, that's him," she said as she reached out and stroked Jac's cheek and jaw with a very soft hand. "Are you still in touch with him?"

"Oh, yes, he is. Unfortunately," said Tony as one of the staff entered and set the tea service on the table. "Thank you, Alice. I'll pour," Tony said, and the young girl gave a slight nod and left the room.

"Tony, tea is good, but I would like some more cognac if you please," said Catherine Marie, Jac's grandmother's sister, Jac great's aunt. Jac had lost both his grandmother and his mother at a very early age, and his aunt Catherine Marie had filled in for the both of them. She had never had any children of her own, and so all the young ones ended up at her spacious home and grounds at one time or another for a stay, but Jac was there with his pals all the time until he went away to high school.

As she said that, an expression crossed her face, and Jac saw his mother and realized just who she was. "Aunt CM," he whispered, and the older lady smiled at him and said in the gentle voice that she had always used to soothe him when he was frightened, "Yes."

Tony poured some brandy into a glass, adding a little ice, watching all the time the scene that was going on in front of him. Jac was hooked on his helping out, and both of them knew it. No matter what this older member of the family asked of Jac, he would do it, and once he started, there was no turning back. Tony quietly left the room after handing the glass of cognac to his aunt Catherine Marie. After about two hours of talking, two cups of tea, and another drink for CM, she drifted off to sleep, and Jac quietly let himself out of the room and the house.

The trip back to the hotel was slow, and Jac's mind was full of thoughts for the favor that CM had finally asked him to do was more in find-and-help detective work instead of the law. It seems that a second cousin of Jac's had defied her parents and had run off with a young man that the family had forbid her to see. Now the parents have disowned the girl and decided to leave her to her own fate. CM said, "That the girl, whose name is Catherine, was my favorite, a good grand niece who I'm terribly worried about." CM wanted Jac to find Catherine and see if she is all right or if she needed any help. Also, CM believed that the young man that Catherine had run off with was from a decent family and would probably be good for her grandniece. If it can be proved that the union is a good one, she would demand that the girl's parents allow the relationship to be accepted and encourage marriage. Jac remembered that CM had an enormous amount of power when it comes to the family's relationships and business dealings. He would not be surprised if that is how his uncle planned to get him back into the family business.

CHAPTER 36

It's show time. That one phrase kept running through Judith's head as they, Princess and she, drove up to the clinic for her appointment with Dr. Frederick Calendar. Was she having second thoughts about this whole procedure? After all, it was she who volunteered for this mission, and she was doing it for KaSandra and all the other women out there whose lives were ruined by Calendar—or did he? A lot of those women would not have their children right now if it had not been for Frederick getting them pregnant with or without the sperm of their husbands. But populating the world with his image is a different subject. Surprise! Yes, Judith told herself this is the right thing to do. *Only you can carry it off, so buck up and put that monster behind bars.*

"You are really quiet," said Princess. "Not getting cold feet are you? We can always do this another day."

"No, I am all right. I am just getting myself psyched up. Frederick can be a very persuasive man, and I really have to focus when around him."

"Good. That's healthy and constructive, and we're here," said Princess.

As Judith and Princess got out of the car, Judith noticed that there was an unusual number of cars in the lot. Judith said to herself, "I wonder why there are so many cars in the lot. The first time I came up here, it was almost empty."

Princess said into her hidden mic, "Did you hear what she said? Be alert for anything." The door opened as they reached it, and a young man and woman came out. She had been crying, and he looked very downcast as they passed the two women.

"Judith, is there more than one doctor in this clinic?" asked Princess.

"No, I believe Calendar works alone but might have student interns other than the nurses work for him." They reached the reception desk, and Judith announced that she was there to see Dr. Calendar, then she asked, "Are there any other doctors in the clinic?"

The young nurse at the desk looked up and smiled. It was not the one Judith had seen before, and she liked this one's countenance much better. "No, Dr. Calendar is the only one, but sometimes, he has interns from the local hospital to observe. Why do you ask?"

"No real reason. I just noticed that the last time I was here, the parking lot was empty, and now, I had a hard time finding a parking space."

"Oh, I'm sorry. Were you told about the parking space behind the clinic?"

"No, but no matter. We are parked now. I am Judith Polymer."

"Yes, Ms. Polymer. The doctor will be right with you. Would you like something to drink? There is coffee, tea, fruit juices, and bottled water over on the far table. Help yourselves."

"Thank you," said Judith and walked to a seat far enough away so she could see what was going on. Princess picked up a hot mug of coffee and a sweet roll, and she said softly, "Judith, say something to me so I'm sure I can hear you while you are in the other rooms."

"One more will bite the dust. Can you hear that?"

"Can I hear what, Judith?" the familiar voice of Frederick asked, making Judith jump.

"Dr. Calendar, you startled me."

"Now, Judith, I thought we were on first name basis."

"Oh, yes, Frederick, and I was just kind of talking to my aunt Jubilee." Frederick looked puzzled, and seeing this, Judith said, "You remember the aunt who gave me the money for this procedure?"

"So you were kind of praying? Now, Judith, I told you, you have nothing to worry about. I'll take the best of care of you." Just then, Princess walked up to the two of them and stood there looking at Judith with a big smile on her face. Frederick turned to look at her and was surprised to see another fascinating looking woman standing so close to them.

"Frederick, let me introduce my best friend, Princess. She's here for my backup support. I hope you do not mind."

"Not at all. Princess, what an extraordinary name," Frederick said while holding Princess's hand in a curious way, which sent warning waves right up her spine.

Princess said, "Papa gave me that name, and it kind of suits me, don't you think?" She was beginning to see what Judith was talking about. She must stay alert around this man. He has an awful kind of charisma.

"I most certainly do," said Frederick, and in his mind, he thought, *I must check this one out further. She would be very interesting just to play around with.* Releasing her hand, Frederick turned to Judith and said, "Now, Judith, if you are ready. Let us get those little eggs of yours so we can start that baby you want so much."

"I'll be right out here, Judith dear, if you need me."

Frederick said, "You are welcomed to keep Ms. Judith company up to the point I'm going to extract her eggs, and then I'll ask you to leave for privacy sake. You understand?"

"Oh yes, and thank you."

Further up the Keys, a tall man with very pale blond hair watched as a motorboat approached him out of the swampy like distance for he could not tell it was near noon due to the overhanging foliage. The boat stopped just at the end of the dock that Kaper was standing on. Two men with Asian features stepped out of the boat and walked slowly toward him. The leader was dressed in an expensive linen suit in a light gray color, a gold shirt, a gray tie with flecks of gold running through it, black leather boots with slightly raised heels. His hair was the color of midnight, but it was starting to gray at the temple and was worn pulled back in a ponytail that hung to his waist. His smile showed white even teeth while giving you the feeling that his smile was put on for your benefit.

The Asian had a briefcase in his left hand and stopped in front of Kaper. He handed the case to his bodyguard to balance. Reaching over with his left hand, he released the box snaps. The lid popped open, and lying in the case were five large bags of white powder. The Asian then took a small knife out of his left hand pocket and made a small cut in the plastic of the top bag, extracting the powder and offered it to Kaper.

Kaper took the knife, dropped the powder into his palm, snapped the lever, closing the knife, and handed it back. Then slowly tasted the coke and nodded his head. Reaching down to the case, which was standing next to his left leg, he opened the case and showed stacks of large bills in twenty neatly tied bundles. The Asian lifted one, flipped through it, and smiled. Then he replaced the bundle, closed the lid, and turned to go. He stopped and turned back to Kaper and said, "Until next time." Before the Asians could reach the motorboat, a bright light was flicked on, which made the surrounding area look like day. There was a man's voice, stating over a bullhorn, "Stay where you are. This is the FBI, and you are all under arrest."

Kaper's arms fell to his side, while the two Asians tried to make a break for it in the motorboat. They were quickly surrounded by other boats and told to cut their engine. *Strange,* thought Kaper as he allowed his hand to be placed in handcuffs. *I tried to get a little ahead, and all that's going to happen to me is that I'm going back prison.*

CHAPTER 37

Judith and Princess got up and walked with Frederick back into the clinic, and as they went, the doctor asked the nurse to get the room ready for Judith's procedure. Then turning to Judith, he said, "Please go with Nurse Shaw, Judith, and I'll see you in just a few minutes."

Judith and Princess entered a large room with an examination table, several chairs, and a stool. Nurse Shaw told her to disrobe, taking off everything, and slip on a gown, then she left without even glancing back.

"Boy, what's her problem. Is she so insensitive she can't even smile?" said Princes. "No wonder that last couple left in tears."

"Oh, you saw that also?" said Judith. "Too bad someone could not explain to them what they are missing if this is the only way they can have a baby."

"They will, sugar. They will," said Princess as she hung up Judith's dress on the hanger she retrieved from the back of the door. As Judith tied the sash on the gown, there was a knock at the door, and Frederick walked in with a big smile on his face.

"Sit, please, the two of you, and I will go over the procedure again for both of you on what I am going to be doing in the next hour. First, Judith, I am going to give you a light injection of lidocaine to relax you and make the lower part of your body a little numb."

"Will I be unconscious?" asked Judith.

"Not at all. You just won't feel as much of the pain when I retrieve your eggs. Just a little pressure is more like it," said Frederick. "So if you are ready," Frederick said, slapping his leg, "we'll get started. Ms. Princess, you can stay with her as she gets sedated, and then you will have to wait in the other room. But I have seen to it that there is some lunch laid out for you."

"Why, thank you, doctor. That is so nice of you to think of me that way," Princess purred in her best southern drawl. After the doctor had left, the nurse returned with a hypodermic needle and seemed to enjoy stabbing into Judith's hip, then she told Judith to relax and left the room.

Princess leaned over to Judith and whispered, "Remember, if that shot makes you too drowsy, just say my name or *help* if anything doesn't seem right to you. I'll be in here in a flash." Then the nurse reappeared and told Princess that she had to leave.

Judith was feeling good all over and not a bit frightened. The door opened, and Frederick walked in and very gently put Judith feet in the strips and separated her legs. Sitting, he said, "Try to relax. Let's see now, Judith, where those beautiful eggs are so I can remove them."

The lidocaine took affect, and Judith did not feel a thing, not even the suction as the doctor removed her eggs from inside her womb. After some time, Frederick said, "There we go. That was not so bad, was it?"

Judith knew that the doctor had said something, but she could not quite make it out for Calendar seemed so far away, but she could see him standing right there next to the examination table. Her mouth seemed so dry that she could hardly form a word to ask him what was wrong with her.

"Don't try to speak right now, Judith, for the shot that you were given paralyzes all the nerves in your body, and the brain cannot get them to react for several hours yet. Nothing to worry about for when you and I are finished, you won't remember much of what happened."

Judith tried to say, "What are you talking about?" But all that came out was a low mumble. Then she saw that the doctor was locking the door, taking off his lab coat, and undoing his trousers. He slipped them off and placed them neatly on the back of the chair.

"You see, Judith, we are going to have a little fun before I let you leave me today. A little payback for the nice lunch we shared a week ago when you looked so lovely." Then Judith saw him remove his jockey shorts and started to climb up on the table on top of her.

She knew that she had to do something to stop this rape. She tried to scream, but nothing come out, so she tried to move her legs out of the stirrups and found that she could not even move her baby toe.

"Relax, Judith, I told you that the brain signals are frozen right now and cannot let the body respond to anything. I know that you can hear everything I am saying for now. But you won't remember when you come out of the medicine."

Judith said *no* and then *help*, and Frederick just laughed and said, "That's not going to help. There is nobody around to even hear that little whisper of yours. Though I am surprised that you could even form the words. Your system must really be in good condition. I'm going to enjoy this."

While Princess was sipping a cup of wonderful tea, she heard that little whisper of help.

Judith's, "Help." Dropping the cup and running toward the back of the clinic, she shouted as she ran, "Did you all hear that help? Judith needs us right now, and I'm going in." She raced past the nurse at the desk and the one sitting outside the operation room that held Judith, and as she approached the door, the nurse said, "Stop. You can't go in there." Princess pushed her out of her way, shouting at the same time, "Police! Out of my way." She hit the door with so much force that it swung open with a shattering sound and smashed against the wall.

Frederick was naked from the waist down and just about to penetrate Judith when Princess broke down the door. "Stop where you are, doctor, and get yourself off that table immediately and away from Judith," Princess said, pointing a gun at Calendar. All Frederick really saw was the gun, a Colt 45, pointing at him, and he froze.

"Down right now," Princess shouted, moving toward Judith as the other officers ran in the room and lifted the doctor off the table. The officer shouted for him to put on his pants. "You are under arrest for attempted rape." The officer started reading him his rights.

Judith was shaking all over and could not stop. She heard Princess and could see her but could not react to what she was saying. "Judith, just lie still, and the police's doctor will be in here in just a minute to see to you. Relax now. It's all over, and Calendar is in custody. He won't be hurting anyone else for a really long time." Judith tried to smile and nodded her head while tears poured from her eyes.

A tall blond woman walked in and smiled at Judith, saying, "Hi, Judith, I am Dr. Martha Vander with the police department of Key West. How are you doing? I'll just take a quick look at you, and then we can get your legs down from these stirrups and check your vital signs before we transfer you to the hospital." While waiting to be taken to Moped Hospital in Key West, Judith was lying on her side with a warm blanket placed over her.

Mike and KaSandra were waiting outside the hospital room that Judith was placed in when Dr. Vander came out. Mike asked, "How is she, doctor?"

"Well, Ms. Polymer is now resting. From the examination that I gave her, she was not raped but a strong drug was used on her, and she may not remember much of what happened to her in the last two hours. I see no reason for her not to be stronger in an hour or so, then you can take her home. She will probably be disorientated for a couple of days, but that should fade."

"Thank you, doctor, for all your help," said KaSandra.

"It is really Ms Polymer that we should be thanking for if she had not acted as bait, Calendar would probably still be abusing women at this moment," said Dr. Vander. She shook hands with both Mike and KaSandra and left to join her group of officers.

Jac had been busy all day and had not heard from anyone when his car phone rang. "Jac, oh good I caught you. This is Kass, and I just wanted to tell you that the sting went well, and Calendar is on his way to police headquarters. Judith was drugged pretty heavily, and we are waiting at the hospital for her to come out of it to take her home."

"Kass, did Calendar hurt her in any way?"

"No, the police doctor checked her out and said she was not raped. Princess got to her just in time. It seems that Dr. Calendar gave her more than a sedative that was supposed to relax her, and Judith had enough awareness to whisper *help*. Princess heard it and kicked down the door just as the doctor was going to penetrate Judith. Wait a minute, Jac. Mike is coming this way." Jac hear a muffled conversation, and then Kass came on the line again. "Jac," she said, "Judith is awake and wants to go back to the hotel, so we will see you later on, right?"

"I hope so, Kass, but if my plans change, I'll call."

CHAPTER 38

Judith, still queasy from the medication, came full awake in her own bed for Mike and Kass had gotten the ambulance to transfer her back to the hotel and rolled her inside without waking her. Opening her eyes, Judith tried to rise, but the room went around so fast the she flopped down again, holding onto the side of the bed for safety. Mike, who had been sitting in a chair next to the bed, reached for her as she flopped and said in his deep voice, "Hold on there, Judith. The doctor said that you were to lie flat for at least four hours until your system gets rid of the medication, or you could fall flat on that pretty face, and we don't want that."

"Oh, Mike. What happened to me? The last thing I remember was the nurse giving me a shot and then Princess telling me she would be right out front. Calendar took off his clothes, and I was trying to get my mouth to work."

"He hit you with the drug called benzodiazepines according to the hospital's lab doctor, and I guess he used that on all of his patients. It immobilizes all of your muscles so you can't move, but you can still hear and see everything that is going on. Then after the drug wears off, the person doesn't remember anything that happened, except that something happened that they didn't like," said Mike.

"Did he..." Judith could not finish the sentence out of embarrassment, and then the room started moving again, making her feel like throwing up.

"No, relax," said Mike. "You are a very strong woman, and you knew that something was wrong. You struggled until you got out *help*, and not only did Princess hear you, but everyone who came running."

"That nurse, Mike, I think her name was Shaw. The one who gave me the shot. She must have known what was in the medication."

"Yes, the police have an all-points bulletin out for her right now, but they think Shaw is an alias. The receptionist told the police that Shaw kept to herself quite a lot and only worked on call for Calendar."

"So do you think she was in on it?" asked Judith.

"That's what the police are going on right now, and they will know more when they check the records file on her and the address she gave. Probably fake, and if I were her, I'd be out of Key West the minute the police knock down the door," said Mike. "Well, enough talk for now I think Joe is about ready to bring up something light for you to eat, and then you must get some more sleep." Before Mike could make it to the door, it was opened, and in walked Joe, who pushed in a cart full of fruit, cheese, little sandwiches without crusts, a serving bowl full of celery soup, and dishes for two.

"Where do you think you are going? Joe asked as Mike made a move for the door.

"I have made enough food here for two, and Ms. Judith cannot eat alone. You know the house rules, Mike. It's a crime in this hotel to let anyone eat alone."

"Ah, what is in the little sandwiches," asked Mike.

"Chicken in my special spread in half, and the rest has ham with small bits of cheese mixed into a spicy Dijon," said Joe.

"I'm staying," said Mike, pulling up a chair to the bed.

Jac had just reached his car at the airport when his phone started ringing. Reaching for it, he said, "Jac."

"Hi, Jac, Kass here. Are you down yet?"

"Yes, I just picked up my car. What's up?"

"Well," Kass continued, "it's Judith. She is still having trouble with the idea that she has to give her testimony for the trial of Dr. Calendar. It's not that she's afraid to tell what she remembers and what led up to us planning the sting; it's what she can't remember that's bothering her. I can't blame her and all those other couples who got their babies and now realize that their son or daughter might be fathered by Calendar. They all took the bribe and kept quiet all these years, and if the word comes out now, Judith's afraid they will back out and not support her claim."

"Where is she now, Kass?" Jac asked as he started the engine of his Porsche.

"In the bar, Judith started feeling better shortly after she ate and didn't want to stay in bed. She insisted that she'd be able to go and check on the bar. Mike and I convinced her to stay only long enough to get everything in order and then go and do something else. You can just tell that she is thinking about what might happen."

"Kass, I'll be there in an hour, and I think we better have a conference with Mike, Tony, if he can make it, Judith, and you and me. We need to settle this situation right now, even if we have to get the four couples subpoenaed if necessary. See if you can arrange the people," said Jac as he hung up and exited the freeway out of Miami and on to the crossways of the Keys.

Mike had been in New York for three weeks now. The circumstances of the death of the senior Kalabrese had never been solved, and it had caught his interest. It was listed as a possible heart attack, but there were too many unexplained questions that the cops considered the case unsolved. Being an ex-cop, he knew about cases going cold. Mike had made a reputation for himself during his years as a cop and still had friends in the business who were willing to talk about anything unusual that was found but not mentioned to the press.

Some of the cop friends of Mike's had thought that Mr. Kalabrese death was a homicide, but they had no way of proving it. They also thought that the son, Kaper Kalabrese, was the one who caused his father's death. They were still interested in finding out how he had done it.

Mike remembered what Jac had told him about Kaper's love for snakes and how his father hated having them around as he was scared to death of them. Mike also wondered if he should mention the reptile skin he found caught in the mat on the floor of the exercise room in Senior Kalabrese's home or wait awhile until he had more proof.

After thinking about the evidence, he decided to keep it to himself until he talked with Jac about his findings. *What would it do to Kaper if it was found out even though it was circumstantial evidence that his father was deathly afraid of snakes.* Mike thought he would also get a hold of Mr. Kenneth Kalabrese's will and see what was left to whom. Kaper had mention in the tape he sent to Jac that his father was much more generous to Jac than to his own son. Had he left something to Jac that he didn't know about yet? He was about to pull up stakes and leave for the airport for his flight back to the Keys when his cell phone rang, and it was Kass, asking him if he was coming back and if so, when he would arrive.

"Yeah, I was just closing up here and heading for the airport. What up?"

"Oh, Jac is driving in from Miami and wanted me to get the group together for a conference. Judith is worried that the four couples are going to back out of convicting Calendar. So I got Tony to come here to the hotel about eight p.m., and that should give Jac enough time to get here, but what about you?" Kass inquired.

"Well, it's five now, and the plane is taking off in about an hour, going right into Key West Airport, so I should be able to make it. If I'm not there right away at eight pm, start without me. Okay?"

CHAPTER 39

The group started gathering together at about 7:45, including Jac who drove in at 7:05 and went directly to his room to change. Tony arrived looking cool and handsome as always and went to the bar to talk with Judith and found Princess still at the hotel.

"I thought you left after they took Calendar off to jail," said Tony.

"Hi to you too," said Princess. "I have a little vacation left, so I decided to take it here. You know that this is not quite finished yet. I'm curious to see how the arraignment turns out and give my friend here some moral support."

Tony tried not to look surprised at Princess's remark. But her forward way of speaking piqued his senses. He started looking her over a little closer and found that he liked what he saw. Princess saw him staring out of the corner of her eye and stopped talking and looked back at him with an encouraging smile on her face.

"I'm still welcomed, aren't I?" Again the blunt and straightforward question gave Tony a hot feeling deep inside.

"As far as I'm concerned, you will always be welcomed in this neck of the woods."

Before he could say more, Jac walked into the bar and was followed by Joe, who stated, "Dinner is ready. There is roast beef or ham, baby squash, Caesar salad, Joe's wonderful apple pie, and then brandy or coffee."

After Joe had left to retrieve the food items, Judith went to the bar for some bottles of wine and glasses. Seeing everyone was settled, Judith opened the gathering with the concerns she had about the parents who were swindled when they find out that Frederick was the sperm donor. Would they be ready for the trial and willing to testify?

Tony said that he was still in contact with all of the couples and would make sure they were on hand if needed, no matter if they got a payoff or not."

"Great," Judith said. "But we do not want them to be hostile witnesses and fair game for the defense."

Tony smiled at Judith and reassured her that it would be his attorneys who would be handling the case and the families. Judith smiled back and thought, *Sure, with your gun against their heads.*

Jac said, "Judith, I think the couples were more afraid when Calendar was out free and able to cause a lot of trouble if they tried anything, but with your testimony alone, he will be going away for a long time, and his license will be revoked."

The discussion went on for another two hours with everyone enjoying the soft breeze off the water, friendship, and full stomachs. Brandy was asked for everyone. The conversation drifted to other matters, and finally, everyone had said good night. Judith stayed for a while and sat, looking at the moon on the water and feeling a lot better about the future trial.

Two days before the trial was to commence, Mike brought word to Jac that there was not going to be any trial. "It seems," he said, "that all four couples got together in New York over the Labor Day holiday and decided amongst themselves to write the court and Judge Henry a letter explaining everything that had happen to them and their part in taking bribes from Dr. Calendar to keep quiet. They also stated that they were all willing to repay the money or take the punishment he thought reasonable to keep their names out of the papers and save themselves and their children from further damage. Hearing this, Calendar, through his attorneys, stated no contest and placed himself in the mercy of the court."

"What does that actually mean?" asked Judith.

"It means the defendant is saying that he is pleading guilty with one exception. The defendant's plea can't be used as an admission of guilt if someone wants to sue him in a civil lawsuit arising out of the criminal act," said Mike.

"I bet his attorneys spread it on thick. How miserable his life was as a kid, and all he really wanted to do was make all the couples happy. With his attorneys' competence, he also probably threw in how many males sperms can be defective, and he knew his were perfect so he saved them money," said Jac.

"Don't worry. When your uncle gets through talking with his old friend Henry, for it seem they went to school together and have worked on different committees for some time, I believe Calendar will get his punishment and not much mercy from the court." said Mike.

"How in the hell did he know about this information so fast?" said Jac.

"Good question. I called you at your office number on my way over here and found it busy, so called Tony next at his home to tell him, and he thanked me but said he already knew," said Mike. "It seems that one of the couples, the Whites, called Tony and told him what they had done, and then they were told that there was not going to be a trial, just a sentencing."

Just then, both men heard glass shattering in the bar and ran to find out what had happened. They found Judith sitting on a bar stool with her hands holding her head and broken glass on the floor around her.

"What the heck happened?" Mike said as he reached Judith. Judith looked up with anger in her dark eyes and said, "I dropped it on purpose. Do you know that sick bastard is not going to trial?"

"Well, yes, but how did you find out so fast?" asked Jac.

"Princess called me from the airport, and it seems that it was on CNN, and she caught it just before she got on the plane. His attorneys were giving some kind of response to the newspaper reporters on the steps of the courthouse about how there was not going to be a trial," said Judith.

Mike asked, "What did they say?" Just then, the hotel phone rang, and Jac picked up the phone and said, "It's from Tony. I'll put him on speaker. Hi, Tony, you are on speaker for Mike and Judith are with me in the bar." Then they all heard Kass's voice as she entered and said, "I'm here too."

"Good, then I don't have to waste time getting a hold of you all," said Tony's strong voice. "You all must have heard CNN by now, and if not, here's what's happening. Calendar has made a deal with the court to give the names of all his patients whom he had impregnated through his sperm and return their money and then leave the country, giving up his citizenship and passport. He will be allowed to sell up and take his belongings to stay out of prison."

"What?" Judith said in a scream, "And the rapes? Are they going unpunished? Sure. Praise the Lord I was not raped, but darn close to it, and what about Kass and all those other women who did not get pregnant because his sperm did not cooperate at the time he raped them?"

"Calm down, Judith," Tony's voice was heard softly over the speaker phone. "What the attorneys didn't say was that the court has not made a decision on the proposal yet. Judge Thomas Henry knows all about the man and is not letting him off lightly. Believe me for there may be a lot more women out there who are too frightened to come forward and complain about the treatment they received at his hands. Judge Thomas wants to consider them also."

"So how long do we have to wait now before there is a decision on what else the bastard is going to get?" said Judith. At the word *bastard*, all the people in the room just stared at Judith in surprise for none of them had ever heard her swear.

Tony just laughed and said, "Will someone give that girl a drink? And in the meantime, I'll tell you what the judge has decided. This won't be made public until Monday, if there is any money left after repayment for what he charged his clients in not giving his services properly; at the cost of two hundred fifty thousand and up for each procedure and the list has been compiled by his attorneys from his records. Then, if there are suits from women who are not on the list because they where too afraid to cause a scandal… To stay out of prison, he has to pay for what can be proven charges of assault or rape at two hundred fifty thousand on each count that is brought against him. That why the judge is allowing some time for women or couples to complain before he closes this case."

"What if he cannot come up with enough money for the charges brought against him?" asked Kass.

"Good question, Kass," said Tony. "That's why the money to stay out of prison is also high. If he can't fulfill the amount, he will have to serve each count that is not paid for in prison and each count of rape or attempted is about ten years."

"Does he even have that much money?" asked Mike.

"I'm not sure how much this man has, but unless a lot of couples and women come out of the woodwork, he just might be able to pay off everything. We will just have to wait a little longer and see the results," said Tony.

"Sorry I have to cut this short, but I'm expecting a guest in about ten minutes. I'll be talking to everyone over there very soon." Then the line went dead.

"I wonder who is dropping in at this late hour." said Mike.

CHAPTER 40

After Mike heard about the Calendar situation he announced that he would be in New York for the next week finishing up on the Senior Kalabrese's case and asked Jac to keep him in the loop on the case. Now Mike was eager to get back to Key West and had one more stop before catching his plane. He drove to the probate court office and asked to check the records for Mr. Kenneth Kalabrese's will. After checking the files, the clerk at the desk said that it was not available and wondered if he could return toward the end of the week. Mike explained to her that he was investigating the case and showed her his license.

"Private detective, are we? Well," she said, "I could probably make a copy for you when it is returned from the desk of my boss and hold it for you to pick up."

Mike smiled back at the very plain and helpful women, and in his best voice, he told her, "See I'm flying out of here in about an hour to Key West, and I'm not sure when I will be returning. It is very important to my case, and if you could mail it to me at this address..." He passed her his card. "I would really appreciate it."

"Well, I don't know."

"I'd be very happy to pay for the copies and the postage, and since I am in New York at least once a month, if you give me your number, I could...well..."

The female clerk knew a line when she heard one, but this detective was so good-looking, she could not help herself. So she took his business card and received the money owed from Mike.

Then just before he left, she gave him her name and telephone number. Mike, on the way out of the courthouse, passed by a flower station and bought a dozen roses and had them sent to a Ms. Char Huette on the seventh floor of Probate Office with a card that said, "See you soon, Mike."

Four days after Mike returned to Key West, the envelope from the New York Probate Office arrived with a copy of Mr. Kenneth Kalabrese's will, and also inside was a note that read, "Thanks so much for the roses. I was the talk of the office for a week. Everyone wanted to know who sent me the flowers and who was Mike."

Mike whistled when he read what Senior Kalabrese had left for Jac. He also wondered why the attorney in charge of the will had not reached Jac by this time for Kenneth had been dead over a year already. He decided to give Jac a call and made an appointment to see him about his findings and the will. Mike had not seen Jac since that night in the hotel when everyone found out the verdict of Dr. Calendar's trial. It seems that Jac's aunt CM had been keeping him pretty busy with some work on her new enterprise, and he hadn't been free for a talk. After letting the phone ring for about six rings, Mike was about ready to hang up when Jac snatched up the receiver and stated, "Scarin."

"Well, old buddy, where have you been?" asked Mike.

"Oh, Mike, I'm sure glad it's you. I have been out of town on business for my great-aunt and just got finished taking her to the airport. I thought maybe her flight was cancelled, and she needed a ride back here," said Jac.

"Where was she going?"

"Catherine Marie is flying back to New York were she is opening a new business in fashion for women her age. I have been up there, making sure everything is set up legally and that she has her funds protected. So what's up with you?"

"I need to have some time with you to fill you in on Kalabrese's murder and his will. What do you say about dinner at The Steak and Fish House at the wharf?"

"Did you say murder?" asked Jac.

"Yes, but I don't want to talk about it on the phone. How about seven?" Mike asked.

"Great," said Jac and hung up.

When Jac arrived at the restaurant, he noticed Mike's silver MG already in the parking lot. He parked the Porsche and walked toward the door, noticing the setting sun as he did so. Jac never got used to the sunsets in the Keys. They were truly breathtaking, especially as the sun sank into the ocean and was always a green-blue tone that time of the day. Mike was sitting in a little bay window, watching the same sunset that Jac had been enjoying minutes ago. There was a bottle of house brew in front of Mike and a stack of half-eaten oysters.

"Hi there, Mike," Jac said as he lowered himself into the booth. "Looks that you started without me."

"Yeah!" Mike grinned. "I had to. I didn't have lunch and was starving. But I saved you a few."

"Mike, you forgot again. I don't eat oyster," said Jac as he watched Mike's face make a grin.

Before Mike could comment, Cheryl, the server, came over to the table to get Jac's order. "Hi, Mr. Scarin. Haven't seen you in quite a while. What would you like?"

"Cheryl, are they serving any crabs tonight?"

"You bet, Mr. Scarin."

"Great. Why don't you bring me an order and another house brew for Mike and me to start with, and we will order our main course in a little while."

After Cheryl had left, Mike popped another oyster into his mouth and smiled at his best friend. "Wait til you see what was just delivered to me from New York's Probate Court," he said as he swallowed. "But first, I have to fill you in on what I learned about Kaper's father's death. I already told you about finding the snake's discarded outer skin in the exercise paddling and that he concealed it from the NY Police for he was certain that they did not know that the senior Kalabrese was deathly afraid of snakes, and I wanted to check with you on when the police should be told." Then he took it out of his sports jacket and laid it on the table between them. Jac, out of the corner of his eye, saw Cheryl coming with their order and dropped his napkin over the specimen bag and leaned back from Mike to let her place the food and drinks on the table.

"You know, you are as crazy as I am sometimes, Mike. You not only concealed evidence from the local NY police but transported it thousands of miles away from the scene of a probable murder."

Mike smiled his sheepish smile and said, "Yeah, I figured it could be more use to you than the police at this time and place. Kaper's father has been dead for over a year now, and his death is considered an unsolved homicide. If Kaper is still trying to pin his death on you, this might just change his mind."

"Very possibly. Mike, you could be right, but while you were in NY, Kaper was picked up here for drug possession with the intent to sell and is now in jail. So what else did you find out from the probate court?" Jac asked.

Mike's look of surprise as he wiped his mouth with his napkin and reached inside a bag that was sitting on the seat made Jac laugh out loud. After gaining his composure back, Mike said, "You will never guess what the senior Kalabrese left you in his will, and it might be another reason why Kaper is so angry toward you." Mike passed the will over to Jac and sat back to watch his expression.

Jac, who had been enjoying his crab, set the leg down and took a sip of beer. "From the look on your face, it must be something nice, but why? That's what I want to know. He was always pitting us against each other, and Kaper always lost something like his car, that time for six months when he lost to me, which was often. It was his personality that crossed him up. Kaper never learned to relax." All this time, Jac was talking to avoid looking at the will. He felt uneasy at what it might say for he never wanted to come between Kaper and his father and always seem to. Reaching across his side of the table, he lifted the sheets of paper and started to read.

The will contained the regular formal words about being in sound mind and so on, and then he read what Kaper had inherited: the house in Manhattan, the condominium in Syracuse, both prime areas of real estate, and a multimillion-dollar business. "With this, he could live two lives," said Jac.

"Sure, but a lot that's going to do him in prison," commented Mike. "But get to the good stuff. The part that states what senior left you." Jac skimmed down and found his name and read, "I also bequeath to Jac Scarin my collection of six classic cars, which are listed in this will, so stated by me in the list of property. Kenneth Kalabrese."

Jac read the same three lines over at least five times before looking up at Mike with a complete bewildered look on his face. "But why?"

"I have a better question for you," said Mike. "Why haven't you been notified of this inheritance by now since Kenneth Kalabrese has been dead over a year, and where are the cars now?"

After asking this question, both men sat silent for quite a while, just eating and thinking their own thoughts. Jac finally broke the silence and said, "I guess I better get a hold of this lawyer of the late Kalabrese and find out what is going on and why I have not been contacted."

CHAPTER 41

Jac took the will back to his office, sat down, and read it through entirely before picking up the phone and calling Job Masterini, an attorney in New York. The phone rang four times, and then a very young woman with Brooklyn accent answered the phone. "Good afternoon. Mr. Job Masterini office. How can I help you?"

"Yes, my name is Jac Scarin, and I would like to talk to Mr. Masterini please."

"Mr. Scarin, Mr. Masterini is in conference right now, but I can have him call you."

"No, that won't do at all. I am calling from Key West, and the matter is about the Kalabrese's will. So if you would be so kind as to slip him a note, I will hold the line."

"I really can't do that, Mr. Scarin, but I will take your information and hand it to him when he is free."

"That's too bad. I just guess I'll have to go to Governor Paterson and suggest that one of his appointed district attorney is involved in a miscarriage of justice." There was complete silence on the other end of the line, and then the young voice said, "Will you wait just a moment?" Then Jac heard channel music while he waited.

Jac waited for two minutes and then heard a click and a gruff voice say, "This is Masterini. What is this matter about that involves Kalabrese's will? And who the hell are you?"

"Is this Mr. Job Masterini?" Jac said.

"Yes, I just said I was."

"I am Jac Scarin of the Scarin family of Boston. I just received the will of Mr. Kalabrese that lists me as a beneficiary. He died over a year ago, and I was not notified that Kenneth had left me anything. I would like to know why and what?"

"Well, Mr. Scarin. I'm sorry I did not recognize your name. I'm also sure that my staff tried many times to contact you and were unable to find out where you lived."

"Hmm, that's amazing that you couldn't find me since a lot of my immediate family still live in New York and of course, Boston. I'm sure any of them would have been very happy to give your staff my number in such a case as a will reading. Now, I suggest that you, Mr. Masterini, hop on a plane and come down here where your staff could not locate me, in Key West, and explain just what happened to my inheritance Mr. Kalabrese left me. Unless you want me to call my friend Thomas Paterson, your wonderful elected governor and a friend of mine, and explain the circumstances to him."

"Mr. Scarin, I would be happy to come down and explain what happened, that you where overlooked. Shall we say in a week's time?"

"No, Mr. Masterini, I would say tomorrow by noon. That should give you enough time to find what is missing and bring it with you. If I don't see you by that time, Masterini, I will call Tom and fill him in on what has happened. Good-bye." Then Jac placed the phone in its cradle.

Jac sat with a slight smile on his face, wondering how Mr. Masterini was going to arrive with six classic cars in his suitcase. He was not counting on even getting one of the cars for he was sure that Kaper had sold the classics at least a year ago to the highest bidder. "Kaper would never let me inherit that much from his father's estate," Jac said out loud.

Masterini drove himself out to the Kalabrese's estate, which was now sitting empty, waiting for a buyer. Driving right up to the garage, he parked, got out, and opened the door with the keys he had. After turning on the light, he found the garage empty, except for a broken-down motorcycle that held the name of Sylvester How. The rest of the name was faded and not legible. He had not remembered the cars being shipped or sold, so he returned to his office to get to the bottom of the situation. Sitting in his spacious office, he pulled the Kalabrese file again and started paging through it. He came upon six bills or sales copies for the six classics cars and a for-sale notice written by a Mr. Jac Scarin to sell all the cars. He did not remember doing any transactions with Mr. Scarin.

Picking up the phone, he called the number Jac had given him, and after Jac answered, he explained what he had found in the file was a letter from Jac stating that he wanted the cars sold. Masterini had checked with his staff and was informed that the cars had gone at auction one month after the death of Mr. Kenneth Kalabrese. The copies of the bill of sales had come in the mail, and the file clerk assumed that Mr. Masterini knew about the sale, and so he put the copies into the Kalabrese file.

"That is very interesting, Mr. Masterini, especially since I just found out that I was even mentioned in Mr. Kalabrese's will two days ago by my associate who obtained a copy of the will from the Probate Office there in New York. Did you investigate the area where the cars were suppose to be stored?"

"Yes, I did, Mr. Scarin. They were stored at the estate's garage. When I drove out yesterday, the garage was empty, except for a broken-down motorcycle with a name that half read Sylvester How. I couldn't read anything else." Jac's head bobbed up as he heard the name Sylvester How, and he said, "I guess you better catch your plane and bring the copies of the bill of sales down here. Hoping there is a sale value on them and someone's name. Oh, and box up the motorcycle, and bring it also. At least I can get a little something out of this."

"You want the motorcycle?"

"Yes, Mr. Masterini. And any other important information that you can bring for I certainly did not write you to sell something I did not even know I had." After Jac hung up the phone, he walked out to the bar area to join Mike for a drink.

CHAPTER 42

"Mike, did you ever hear of a motorcycle with the name of Sylvester How something?"

Mike's head moved so fast that Jac thought it was going to roll off his neck. "Did you say Sylvester?"

"Yes. It seems that all that was left in the garage at the Kalabrese's estate was an old broken down Sylvester How. I'm having Mr. Masterini bring it with him when he arrives tomorrow with the copies of the bill of sales for the six cars that I was suppose to have inherited and supposedly sent a notice to sell all the cars at auction."

"What?" said Peter from behind the bar, where he was stacking liquor bottles, "How can that be if you didn't even know about the inheritance until a month ago when Kaper told you on that tape?" said Peter.

"That is a good question, Peter, but I have a better one. What about this Sylvester How?" Mike asked. Jac started to smile as he saw the look on Mike's face again.

"It seems that the bike was in such bad shape that the only name Mr. Masterini could get off of it was Sylvester How. Well, do you realize what that bike might be?" Mike's voice rose up a whole octave.

"Wait, wait!" said Peter. "What am I missing here?"

Jac was now grinning so wide that he almost choked on his drink as he swallowed. "Now, wait a minute, Mike. We don't know if it is or not."

"Know what?" said Peter again. "What are you two talking about?"

Mike put down his glass and looked at Peter. "You are too young to know about a motorcycle by the name of the Sylvester Howard. Back in the 1820, I think, this man called Sylvester Howard Roper built a motorcycle, and there were only a few of them made of this type. There are people out there who would pay more money than all those classical cars Jac was supposed to inherit put together. They are worth a fortune in any shape to some buyers, just to get their hand on a Sylvester Howard."

"Wow," was all that Peter could say.

"Jac, if that bike is a Sylvester, then the laugh is on Kaper," said Mike.

EPILOGUE

Dr. Calendar was unable to come up with the full amount of money needed to keep him out of prison for ten more women came forward and explained that they had medical bills as proof of being under Dr. Calendar's medical procedure. Five never returned for the final in vitro procedure and could not remember or explain how they got pregnant on that one visit but were happy with their babies. The other five names found on the list that was given to the court put in a claim after they were informed of the circumstances. Frederick had found enough money to pay off five of the ten women who come forward.

The sentence for rape in most states is six to seven years. He was sentenced to thirty years, which was reduced to twenty, and upon release, his licensed would be revoked in the U.S., and he would have to leave the country and never return or he may go back to prison to finish his sentence.

Kaper was sent back to prison with a reduced sentence of two to five years thanks to his lawyer, who convinced the jury that he was not going to sell the coke but use it himself to relieve his pain on the loss of his beloved father a year ago.

Jac kept the information about the snake skin and its existence quiet in case Kaper decides to start his hostilities again upon his release, then Jac could put a final end to this vendetta and send him packing.

Jac Michael Scarin was already nine months old and standing by himself. He was walking from a chair to whatever would hold him up, and he was quite proud of his accomplishments. Jac had asked Kass to marry him and allow him to adopt JM. So they were married in a quiet service with all their friends in attendance. The reception was held at the hotel, and Joe Flowers catered the whole affair.

On a quiet night, just after Jac and Kass were married, the two of them sat on the balcony, enjoying the sunset and a wonderful glass of champagne. The telephone rang, and a man who introduced himself as Sergeant Sean Mahoney of the New York Police Department told Jac that a Kaper Kalabrese had escaped on his way to prison and was on the loose. Jac thanked the sergeant for informing him and hung up. Looking at Kass, he said, "Well, here we go again. Kaper escaped on his way to prison."